Spirit Of The Wild Horse

Wild Horse Westerns
Book 2

By
Duane Boehm

Spirit Of The Wild Horse: Wild Horse Westerns Book 2

Copyright 2018 Duane Boehm

For more information or permission contact: boehmduane@gmail.com

ISBN: 1-98627-595-7

Other Books by Duane Boehm

In Just One Moment
Last Stand: A Gideon Johann Western Book 1
Last Chance: A Gideon Johann Western Book 2
Last Hope: A Gideon Johann Western Book 3
Last Ride: A Gideon Johann Western Book 4
Last Breath: A Gideon Johann Western Book 5
Last Journey: A Gideon Johann Western Book 6
Last Atonement: A Gideon Johann Western Book 7
Where The Wild Horses Roam: Wild Horse Westerns Book 1
Wanted: A Collection of Western Stories (7 authors)
Wanted II: A Collection of Western Stories (7 authors)

Dedicated to Aunt Pat for helping me believe in this crazy journey

Prologue

Cimarron, New Mexico Territory

May 27, 1866

Sixteen-year-old Levi Bolander couldn't help but amble along with his head down and his shoulders slumping. The last day of school before the summer break had him in a melancholy mood. He loved going to class, and even with all the obstacles life had thrown him, he still had designs of someday becoming a lawyer—a seed planted years ago by his now-deceased mother.

When Levi was twelve years old, he had returned home from school one day and found his parents and little brother and sister massacred by Indians. The sight of their mutilated bodies still gave him nightmares that caused him to wake up screaming at all hours of the night. His mother's brother had taken him in after that. Uncle Eldon hadn't offered his home out of any great love, but merely because he got to shirk doing any cooking or cleaning whatsoever for the meager amount of food he provided Levi.

As Levi walked along the road, he held out hope that by the time he returned to the cabin his Uncle Eldon would be passed out from hitting the bottle early that day. Uncle Eldon despised Levi "wasting" his time attending school when he could be out working. He also hated the boy's long, curly hair. Levi's momma had loved her son's locks, and he continued to wear it how she'd liked it, wishing to keep one memory alive as others faded with time.

Levi spied his uncle sitting on the porch in a straight-backed chair tilted on two legs against the wall. Uncle Eldon's trusty jug sat beside him with the cork removed.

His uncle wasn't a tall man, but what he lacked in height he made up for with a barrel chest. He didn't believe in baths. His hair always looked greasy, and he didn't smell much different than a pig. Uncle Eldon had been the black sheep of the family, and Levi's mother had kept him away from her children as much as possible.

"Don't come into this yard looking all hangdog just because school's finished and you'll have to start working like a man," Uncle Eldon bellowed as he lowered his chair onto all four legs.

"No, sir, Uncle Eldon. I'm ready to go to work," Levi replied.

"Good thing. Barney is expecting you at his blacksmith shop good and early tomorrow morning," his uncle warned.

Levi had spent the last two summers working for the blacksmith. The job was miserably hot and tiring. Some days his clothes were so drenched in sweat that he looked as if he had jumped into a river. Barney's disposition was only slightly less hateful than Levi's uncle's—the blacksmith issued orders with the bark of a sergeant. Though the boy's wiry frame didn't reveal its strength, the work had made him as strong as most full-grown men. He was able to hold his own against nearly anyone. He'd long ago silenced any boy in school who dared tease him about his hair.

"Yes, sir," Levi answered in an attempt to appease his uncle.

"Get on inside and start fixing supper. I'm hungry," Eldon ordered before taking a swig of whiskey and reclining his chair back against the wall.

After Levi entered the cabin, he set his schoolbooks on the table and began shoving kindling into the stove. Once he had the stove hot, he carved off a couple chunks of salt pork and tossed them into the skillet along with some sliced turnips.

The pork was just beginning to sizzle good and give off some aroma when Uncle Eldon staggered into the cabin. Levi looked over his shoulder at his uncle and knew that he had no chance of making it through the evening without trouble. Uncle Eldon had that belligerent scowl on his face that always preceded violence. His uncle walked to the table and, with a sweep of his arms, sent the books flying halfway across the room.

"I don't know what Sally was thinking putting notions in your head about schooling. Of course, she always was a dreamer with fancy ideas about living. The only thing a man needs to know how to do is sign his name and a little ciphering so he don't get cheated," Eldon yelled.

"Please don't talk about Momma that way," Levi said.

"Don't you be sassing me. I'll talk about my sister any way that I want to. She's the fool who got herself killed by savages and left me with the heavy burden of raising you. You should heed what I say over some whim you carry around from a ghost," Eldon screamed in his drunken agitation.

Levi didn't reply. He gave his uncle a hard stare.

"I think maybe it's time I cut that hair of yours. Make you look like a real man instead of a little girl. I think your momma must have wanted you to be a frilly little thing. Maybe you want to be a pretty boy for other men," Eldon said with a scoffing laugh as he approached Levi.

As his Uncle Eldon neared Levi, the drunkard reached for the knife he wore in a sheath on his belt. Levi shoved his uncle hard before the weapon could be retrieved. Eldon stumbled backward a couple of steps, then charged the boy. A right hook connected with Levi's cheek, knocking the boy against the stove. As Levi caught himself, the heat of the cast iron sent shooting streaks of fire through his hands. He grabbed the searing skillet and swung it wildly into his tormenter's skull with a sickening thud. Uncle Eldon's legs buckled, and he dropped to his knees. He shook his head a couple of times like a stunned mule, then pulled his knife as he stood back up.

"You're going to die. I'll make you scream like the little girl you are," Eldon yelled as he charged like a raging bull.

Levi willed himself to grab the blistering-hot skillet again. In a desperate attempt at self-preservation, he jumped to the side wielding the frying pan. He swung it against his uncle's head just as the knife plunged into his upper left arm. Levi gritted his teeth and refused to acknowledge even a hint of the pain the knife had inflicted while his uncle teetered before him with a blank stare. Four years of enduring beatings and belittling had unleashed a long-simmering rage that the boy no longer wished to corral. Levi backhanded the skillet into his Uncle Eldon's face and watched as he collapsed onto the floor, his nose pancaked against his cheeks. Eldon's body began twitching all over, and he let out a wail that made the hairs on the back of Levi's neck stand on end.

"Oh God, he's dying," Levi moaned as he dropped the skillet and stared at his uncle.

Levi probed his own wound with his fingers before ripping his sleeve from his shirt. He fetched a kerchief from his pocket and tied a tourniquet around his arm, using his teeth and good hand to knot it. As he wiped his sticky hands on his already-blood-speckled pants, he glanced around the room. His mind raced so fast that his thoughts were no more than jumbled nonsense. He didn't know what to do next, so he sat down at the table. His chest felt as if an ox was sitting on it, and he wondered if he might suffocate as he tried to fill his lungs with air.

"You just have to relax and breathe," he said aloud to himself.

Levi sat at the table a good ten minutes taking slow, deep breaths until his mind gained some clarity. He had no idea whether what had just happened would be considered self-defense. In fact, he wasn't sure if he had defended himself or had provoked the fight. Everything had happened so fast that the events were all a blur. The only option that seemed feasible was to run.

He walked over to the water bucket and scrubbed away the blood from his hands. The cool water felt good on his burned palms, so he soaked them for couple of minutes before changing into clean clothes. He caught sight of the revolver hanging in its holster from a peg on the wall and strapped it on. The belt felt awkward and cumbersome around his waist. He'd only shot the pistol a few times—when his uncle had been in an unusually generous mood.

As he pulled the revolver from the holster, Levi said, "I better learn how to shoot with this thing. Pa always said that wearing one and not knowing what you are doing is more dangerous than not wearing one at all." He felt silly for having a conversation with himself and looked around the room as if to see whether Uncle Eldon might be watching him. To his surprise, his uncle raised his head off the floor.

"I'll kill you if it's the last thing I ever do," Uncle Eldon moaned.

With the gun still dangling from his hand, Levi walked over to his uncle. He pointed the weapon at him, contemplating putting a bullet into his nemesis's head. His uncle stared at him unflinchingly and with contempt. Hatred overwhelmed Levi's senses, but he didn't have the will for cold-blooded murder.

"I knew you couldn't do it. You're just a big sissy," Eldon sneered.

Levi reared his leg back and then drove the toe of his boot into his uncle's temple, snapping the drunk's head sideways and knocking him unconscious again.

His uncle's saddlebags had been carelessly tossed into a corner of the cabin. Levi stuffed them with clothes, a hunk of salt pork, several raw turnips, and all the ammunition they had. Not having a cent to his name, Levi reluctantly retrieved the can above the fireplace where his uncle kept whatever little money he'd accumulated. He found three half eagle five-dollar pieces and a few other coins and stuffed them into his pocket. A well-worn copy of *David Copperfield* had landed askew against the hearth. Levi's teacher, Miss Martin, had given him the book that very day to have something to read throughout the summer. He gazed at the novel for a moment before shoving it into a saddlebag, too. On the way out the door, he grabbed the rifle and headed to the dilapidated shed where his uncle kept his horse. The animal wasn't much to look at and would never hold up if a posse hounded him, but riding beat walking. He saddled the gelding and led him out into the yard.

"God have mercy on my soul," Levi said as he gazed at the cabin.

He wondered why bad luck hung over him like a cloud—or maybe *he* was just plain bad luck. Everybody he had ever cared for had died. Uncle Eldon was a miserable human being, but nonetheless, Levi longed to feel some remorse for the beating he had given the man. The only emotions he could summon were relief that his living hell had ended and then anger that his dreams of becoming a lawyer were surely as dead as his family. He wished he had his momma to hold him and tell him everything would be fine, like when he had been a little boy with a skinned knee.

With no idea where to go, he headed out on the road that ran north, away from town.

Chapter 1

The mountains near Empire City, Colorado

September 3, 1877

Ellis Shuman bellowed at his two cousins, Harper and Jordan. Levi kept his distance and a wary eye on the proceedings. The men had never drawn weapons on each other, but such a thing eventually happening seemed inevitable. Levi noticed Ellis's squaw, Bluebird, sneak into the safety of the cabin. As usual, she was the source of the argument. The topic came up whenever the men had sat around drinking too much. Ellis had won the Laguna Pueblo woman from Mexicans in a card game down in the New Mexico Territory, and the cousins thought he should share her with them.

The notion of sharing a woman with family disgusted Levi; the irony that he occasionally traveled to whorehouses to pay for a woman shared by countless men was lost on him. The memory of seeing his massacred family also caused Levi to hold a deep hatred for all Indians, even if he begrudgingly had to admit that Bluebird looked pretty and carried herself with a certain dignity in spite of her circumstances. Her piercing brown eyes seemed to look right through a person, and her elegant nose and full lips gave her a graceful appearance that was easy on the eyes. She usually wore a deerskin outfit that she'd made after her two cotton dresses had worn so thin as to be practically see-through. Bluebird was small in stature, but she could work all day and never grow tired. The only sound she ever made was an occasional scream when Ellis worked her over good. He liked to take his anger out on Bluebird, though he was careful never to leave more than bruises or maybe a busted lip. He wasn't about to disfigure his prize possession. Levi always turned his head rather than watch the beatings. He kept his mouth shut, figuring if Ellis wanted to beat his Indian, it was his business.

An outlaw by the name of Pete Lawson had discovered this hideout years ago and had built a cabin on the spot. It proved ideal for avoiding the law with its single narrow entrance and lookout points all around the perimeter. Levi and the Shumans had ridden with Pete at separate times in the past. After Pete's untimely death at the end of a hangman's rope, the men had returned to the cabin to take refuge in an uneasy alliance. Levi didn't trust the Shumans any farther than he could throw them, so he made a point never to drink so much as to be unable to defend himself. The three men were unruly and mean, but Levi had practiced his shooting around them enough to give them a healthy respect for his ability with a gun. They had yet to challenge him.

"What are you looking at?" Harper yelled at Levi after again losing the argument with his cousin. He pulled his knife from his belt and stumbled toward Levi.

"Harper, you best stay away from me. I'm not in the mood for you," Levi warned as he retrieved his own knife from its sheath and stood.

"Get back over here," Ellis ordered his cousin.

"Do you think I'm scared of that scrawny thing? He thinks he's better than us 'cause he has some schooling and can use big words. I'm tired of it. I aim to do me a little cutting to teach him to be a mite friendlier around here," Harper boasted.

Harper began poking the air with his knife as he approached. Levi stood motionless with his weapon held ready. Once Harper was within a step of him, Levi slashed his knife with the swiftness of a cat pouncing on a mouse. The blade cut across Harper's chin, slicing it open to the bone. Harper let out a bloodcurdling scream that made Levi wince. The outlaw dropped his knife and grabbed his face as he stumbled backward and fell.

"Bluebird, bring out your sewing kit," Ellis yelled.

"I'll kill him if he ever comes at me again," Levi warned.

"There won't be no next time," Ellis said as he examined his cousin's chin.

Ellis sat on Harper's chest and Jordan held his brother's head as Bluebird sewed the wound shut. The screaming got so bad that Levi couldn't stand to listen to it any longer. He saddled his horse.

"I'll be back in whenever you see me," Levi said as he rode away.

Levi preferred to work alone. He tended to rob settlers on their journey out West. The payoff wasn't nearly as good as what the Shumans hauled in, but he got by. The law also never got very concerned over some greenhorns losing a few valuables. Ellis and his cousins usually held up stagecoaches or pay wagons. They were big on the notion that dead men don't talk. Levi prided himself on the fact that he had never killed anyone. To his way of thinking, if he let his victims live, he provided them with the opportunity to earn back whatever valuables they had lost. His flawed reasoning allowed him to sleep at night and not to think too deeply about the life he had fallen into since running away from his uncle.

He seldom thought back to the period when he lived with his uncle or to the happy days with his family. Sometimes he even had a hard time remembering what his momma had looked like. All those good memories seemed like a lifetime ago—and somebody else's life. Now he just lived day to day, with no hope or joy.

Traveling through the mountains toward the plains was slow going. Levi usually rode to where settlers from the east arrived from across the prairie, seeking their fortunes. He would rob enough of them to make the trip worth his while.

After bypassing Empire City, he made it to the outskirts of Idaho Springs. His resolve to continue his journey began to sag once he spied a saloon in the booming mining town. He tied up his horse and entered the establishment. The place was filled with rambunctious miners spending their hard-earned money to drink away their miseries for a while. All the laughter and shouting—as well as a piano player pounding the keys for all he was worth—almost overwhelmed Levi's senses. He ordered a beer and stood at the bar, minding his own business as he sipped his brew.

A giant miner came up next to him. He reached over and tousled Levi's hair.

"Hey there, curlylocks. You got awfully pretty hair," the miner said in a booming voice to draw attention. He belly laughed and fluffed Levi's hair again.

Levi had been through such taunting more times than he cared to recall. It wasn't as if he was the only man with long hair in Colorado, but the curls and his wiry frame seemed to make him an easy target. "Just let me drink my beer and leave me alone."

The miner reached for Levi's hair again. "You're kind of sensitive, like a girl, aren't you?"

With a quick spin, Levi drove his knee into the miner's groin. As the giant doubled over in pain, he windmill-punched him in the face, sending the miner to the floor. Levi rested his hand on his revolver. "Anybody else got something to say?" he yelled.

The saloon went silent as the last note of the piano faded away. Nobody answered him. The miner lay curled up at Levi's feet in a fetal position with his hands tucked into his crotch. Levi grabbed his beer and dumped it on the man's head before walking out of the saloon. He saw a barbershop across the street and contemplated getting his hair cut off, but he mounted his horse instead and headed back in the direction he had come.

A small trading post sat on the outskirts of town. As Levi neared the store, he noticed there were no horses tied outside. He wondered if any miners were in the establishment. The thought of returning to the hideout empty-handed weighed heavily upon him. Normally, he wouldn't attempt a robbery so close to the hideout, but he felt so low that he didn't care. His ambivalence emboldened him. He tucked his hair into his hat and pulled his bandanna up over his nose. With his revolver drawn, Levi burst through the door. Three miners were standing at the counter, chatting with the clerk. They turned at the loud noise and eyed the masked man.

"Charge him. He can't get all of us," one of the men hollered. As if taking orders from a general, the miners rushed Levi.

"Stop," Levi yelled as he fired his Colt into the floorboards.

The bullet ricocheted and nicked the shin of one of the men. He let out a war whoop that stopped the other two in their tracks. They watched their friend hopping on one leg as if he'd invented a new dance. Levi got so caught up in all the commotion he barely noticed, out of the corner of his eye, the clerk raising a shotgun. He dove into an aisle as the gun roared, sending canned goods flying through the air and showering him in a rain of beans. Levi bolted for the door and made it outside before the clerk could reload. He galloped away, hearing the boom of the shotgun ring out again just as he rode out of range of the pellets.

Levi slowed his horse. He figured a posse would be on its way soon, and he needed to be smart about not wearing down the animal. He had a fine mount and felt certain he could stay ahead of the men if he traveled wisely. Back in his younger days, he had a sorry horse that he rode too hard, and a sheriff had caught him after he'd committed a robbery. As luck would have it, he had managed to hide the money he'd stolen before his capture. Lack of evidence and his victim's inability to identify him had forced the chagrined sheriff to release him—after three days in jail. After that episode, he'd saved up some money and bought the best horse he could find.

Humiliation began to set in as he thought about being thwarted by three miners and a clerk. He knew he could have shot all three miners before they reached him if he had any stomach for killing. Lots of practice had made him an accurate shot and fast with his gun, but his unwillingness to use it had just about got him killed. Doubts about his ability to live a life of crime began to creep in as he let his horse walk up a steep grade. He put the animal into a lope once he crested the hill and started down the other side. At the faster pace, he didn't catch wind of himself so much. The bean juice made him smell like a bad fart.

After riding a good while, he stopped at the top of a steep incline to take in the view of the land behind him. He could see for miles. With the aid of his spyglass, he spotted five riders in the distance, not far from the edge of Idaho Springs. The rough terrain would make it impossible for them to catch him as long as he kept moving.

Levi arrived back at the hideout at dusk, feeling lower than when he had left. The sight of the Shumans sitting in their usual spot in the yard, passing a jug around, made him wonder why he had bothered to return. Harper's jaw looked badly swollen. The wound was an angry red. The three of them eyed Levi with contempt as he approached.

"That was a quick trip," Ellis said.

"I'm going to go to bed. Keep it down," Levi ordered, ignoring the comment as he climbed off his horse and faced the Shumans.

"You might never wake up," Harper mumbled, unable to move his jaw much to talk.

"Ellis, you better control your cousin. The next time will be a lot worse than a sliced chin. Nothing has gone right today, and I'm plenty irritable," Levi warned.

"I'll keep an eye on him. You smell bad," Ellis noted.

Levi sighed loudly and marched toward the cabin. He let out snort at the irony that a man whose idea of a bath was getting caught in a rainstorm had just called him out for stinking. As he dropped onto his cot, he wondered how much farther his life could sink.

Chapter 2

Langley Ranch near Fort Laramie, Wyoming Territory September 4, 1877

All of Caroline Langley's antsy behavior was starting to get on Caleb Gunnar's nerves. Caroline's mother, Claire, and Claire's soon-to-be husband, Joey Clemson, looked as if they were growing weary of the young rancher's antics, too. As Caroline buzzed around the room, the three others sat at the kitchen table. They were watching her as if she was a troublesome bumblebee.

"Would you please calm down? I'm sure that meeting my parents will go as well as it did the first time," Caleb said in an attempt at humor.

Caroline's initial encounter with Caleb when he had interviewed for a job had been nothing short of a disaster. She had only hired him after he had wilily backed her into letting him attempt to break a horse because she had challenged his Southern heritage. After he successfully rode the horse, she had no choice but to employ him.

Caleb had received a telegram from his parents two days prior, informing him that their train had arrived in Cheyenne and they would reach Fort Laramie by stagecoach that evening. He and Caroline were planning to leave that afternoon to go to town to get them.

"That's not funny. I want them to like me," Caroline said as she plopped into a chair next to Caleb.

"Just be yourself and they will love you just like I do," Caleb said.

Claire gave her daughter a stern look. "Caroline, calm yourself. The only reason they won't like you is if you continue to act as you are now. They'll think you're addlebrained," she warned.

"I know. I've gotten myself all worked up for no reason," Caroline replied.

Joey drained the last of his coffee and set the cup down on the table a little harder than he meant to do. "I've got to get busy. Caroline, you'll be fine. By the way, you look nice in that new dress." He stood, picked up his hat from the table, and left the kitchen.

"I don't know if I can stand wearing dresses the whole time they are here. I feel like a fraud for doing so," Caroline lamented.

Caroline's usual attire consisted of men's clothing. She had begun dressing in such a manner after her father's death, when she began to run the ranch. Dresses now felt as foreign to her as trousers had once. On a recent trip to town, she had bought three new dresses, and her mother had made her three more.

"I already told you that you should wear whatever you want around here," Caleb said.

Rolling her eyes, Caroline said, "I'll just be glad when it is time to leave to go get your parents so we can get this over with."

"I'll certainly be glad to meet Mr. and Mrs. Berg," Claire said.

Claire emphasized the surname to make sure Caroline and Caleb knew that she was still a bit miffed that she had only recently been informed that Caleb's last name, Gunnar, was an alias he'd taken after running from Tennessee for fear he wouldn't get a fair trial after killing his brother-in-law in self-defense. She'd recently found out she had been kept in the dark until it was certain the Bergs were coming, and that had hurt her feelings. It gave her the impression that the others didn't think she could be trusted with a secret. Even Joey had been in on keeping her uninformed. Her high opinion of Caleb certainly hadn't changed with the news, but she didn't appreciate the way things had been handled.

"Mother, how many times do I need to apologize? I'm sorry we didn't tell you sooner, but with all we had already dealt with around here in the spring, I didn't want to give you something new to worry over," Caroline said.

Earlier that year, a rancher named Nathan Horn had attempted to destroy the family's livelihood by killing mustangs that the Langleys used for breeding. They supplied horses to the army and area ranchers. An attempt had even been made on Caroline's life. The matter had been settled when Caleb and Joey had killed Nathan and his son, along with their ranch hands, to put an end to their quest for control of the open range.

"I suppose, but I still feel as if you think I'm too fragile for the truth. I have things to do now," Claire said as she darted out of the room.

"I told you we should have told her a long time ago," Caleb said to Caroline.

"I could still fire you," Caroline said with a mischievous lilt in her voice. "Let's go brush the horses and check their feet to get our minds off everything."

After returning from the barn and eating a quick lunch, Caleb and Caroline rode into Fort Laramie and rented a two-seat carriage and a team of horses. They tied their mounts behind the rig and killed time shopping as they waited for the stage to arrive. Caroline's nerves began to get the better of her again, and she became quite chatty. Caleb, in an attempt to silence her, bought a sack of licorice with the hopes that the chewy laces would occupy her mouth with something other than speech. The treat proved halfway successful, though Caroline valiantly continued attempting to talk as she anxiously crammed in the candy.

As the stagecoach came into sight, Caleb pulled a kerchief from his pocket and handed it to Caroline. "You better rub your teeth, or my parents are going to think you have a rotting set of choppers."

"Oh my God. I didn't think about that. Why did you buy me licorice?" Caroline whined before vigorously scrubbing her mouth.

"I wanted to give you something to chew on besides my ear," Caleb said, prompting a scowl from his wife-to-be.

Caleb and Caroline stood waiting as the passengers climbed out of the stage. Olivia Berg let out a small cry at the sight of her son. She rushed into his arms and began sobbing. Nils Berg awkwardly patted his son's back as he waited for his wife to regain her composure.

"Daddy, Momma, I'd like you to meet Caroline Langley," Caleb said after his mother let him out of her crushing embrace. He made a quick swipe of his eyes with his sleeve and beamed with pride at his fiancée.

Olivia faced her future daughter-in-law. "Well, you are a pretty little thing. You look just like I imagined. Please excuse my behavior. I became a little overwhelmed seeing Caleb. There was a time when I never thought I'd lay eyes on him again," she said before hugging Caroline.

Nils offered his hand. "Pleased to meet you," he said.

"I'm so glad to finally meet you both. How was the trip?" Caroline asked. Her nervousness had dissipated with the meeting. She could already tell she would like Caleb's parents.

"The train ride was wonderful—the stagecoach not so much. Two days is more than a person should have to bear in one of those things," Olivia said.

"I've never seen so much flat land as on the train ride. Now, by contrast, these mountains are something to behold," Nils added.

Olivia reached up and touched Caleb's cheek. "I'm so happy to see you again."

"Let's get you to the ranch. I'm sure you're both exhausted," Caleb said as he shepherded his parents toward the carriage.

The ride back to the Langley home gave Caroline an opportunity to get to know Caleb's parents. She felt completely at ease around them and their down-to-earth ways. She spent most of her time telling stories about Caleb that underscored her belief he might be the most opinionated and hardheaded man she had ever come across in her life. Caroline went into minute detail about the time they negotiated breeding terms for using Caleb's stallion, Leif, and how they both insulted each other before the transaction was completed. Olivia agreed with the assessment of her son, telling of childhood incidents that confirmed the women's viewpoint. These caused both to giggle with joy at Caleb's expense.

Claire had prepared an early dinner, and Joey had the table set by the time the carriage arrived at the ranch. After the introductions were out of the way, Claire ushered everyone to the dining room. She served steaks, baked potatoes, and green beans. An apple pie waited nearby, cooling for dessert.

Nils farmed and bred horses back in Tennessee, so his interest in the ranch's horses dominated the conversation as the others informed him of the challenges of raising animals in the West. He was also anxious to see Leif, the prized stallion that he had given his son to help him escape the law back home. Once the meal was finished, Joey and Caleb led Nils to the barn.

"Looks like Wyoming agrees with Leif," Nils said as the horse nuzzled him. He patted the horse's neck and eyed the condition of the prized animal.

"Everything agrees with Leif—as long as he has a string of girlfriends," Caleb said.

After spending a few minutes with the horse, Nils said, "Show me some of those mustangs I've heard so much about."

The men walked to a pasture containing horses the ranch hands were still in the process of training. By that time, the sun had sunk well to the west, highlighting the glinting coats of the animals as well as the mountains to the north.

"Now that's pretty. Son, I see why you fell in love with this land. It's hard to beat a place with fine horses and scenery like what's over your shoulder. I wouldn't have missed this for the world," Nils said.

"I'm glad you like it, Daddy," Caleb said.

"I like that Caroline, too. She's a lively little thing. I can see why you were drawn to her," Nils said.

Caleb glanced at Joey, and the men exchanged knowing smiles.

"She's kind of like whiskey—an acquired taste. We couldn't even stand each other until we didn't," Caleb said with a laugh.

Joey gave Nils a tap on the arm and a wink. "They might not have known how they felt about each other, but everybody else on the ranch sure did. Every time they were together, the sparks flew like a roaring campfire in a windstorm."

"He's happier than I've seen him in a long time. Those dark clouds that hung around him are gone now," Nils noted.

"Yes, they are. I watched them blow away," Joey said.

After Caleb's wife and baby had died during birth a few years ago, he had really thought the rest of his life would be just going through the motions of living. No small part of his current state of happiness was the result of a chance encounter with Joey.

Caleb could feel his face turning red. "You know I'm standing right here and can hear both of you. You could have had the decency to have this conversation behind my back. We better get to the house before the women get to telling stories on all of us."

Chapter 3

The seamlessness with which the families bonded exceeded Caroline's rosiest expectations, but all the togetherness quickly started to wear on her. She needed some time with Caleb. The only moments she'd been alone with him happened when they were working horses together. Even then, they barely had time to talk. When her mother came up with a plan for everybody to travel to town for a meal at the hotel, Caroline saw her opening. She begged off with the excuse that she and Caleb needed to check on the mustangs on the open range. Joey had raised his eyebrows in surprise and suppressed a smirk. As ranch foreman, he knew she was full of beans. Besides, Dan and Reese, the ranch hands, could have easily performed the task. She cut her eyes at him with the hope of keeping him silent. Claire appeared disappointed at her daughter's plans but didn't make a fuss.

Caleb and Caroline went to the barn with the purpose of brushing horses and readying the rented carriage for the others to take their trip into town. As Joey, Claire, and the Bergs climbed into the buggy, Olivia lamented that the young couple were unable to accompany them. Joey gave Caleb a sly wink before popping the reins and departing.

The young couple had never had a chance to have the house to themselves before now. They all but ran from the barn into the home the moment the carriage disappeared out of sight. Caleb swooped Caroline up into his arms and carried her to her bedroom as his bride-to-be let out a giggle. All of their previous lovemaking had taken place outdoors, sometimes in less-than-ideal conditions. With all the time in the world and the comfort of a bed, they didn't feel the need to rush their pleasure as they normally did. That day, there was no fear of being spied upon or a need to hurry because it felt too darn chilly.

After they made love, Caroline pulled the sheet up to her chin and let out a giggle. "In just a little over a week I'll be Mrs. Gunnar," she said.

"Yes, you will," Caleb said as gave her a kiss. "Do you think all four of us can live in this house and not go crazy?"

"I think we can manage until we build our house in the spring. George and I lived here, and it wasn't bad. Of course, he wasn't near as amorous as you," Caroline said with a smile.

George was Caroline's first husband. They had divorced after he ran off with some harlot from Fort Laramie. The ordeal had left Caroline bitter and unhappy. She had been nearly intolerable to deal with before Caleb came along and made her believe in love again.

"Well, you're going to have to be a lot quieter than you just were," Caleb teased.

Caroline smacked Caleb's arm and turned red. "Caleb."

Caleb let out a laugh that shook the bed. "I looked at your parents' old cabin the other day. It's still in good shape—except for all the odds and ends that have been stored in it. We could move into it."

"I don't think so. I'll take the comforts of this house and learn to be quiet," she said with a wink.

"Everybody seems to be getting along quite well," Caleb said.

"Yes, they are. Your mother is so reserved and mine is so audacious. I feared they would be oil and water, but they seem to really enjoy each other's company. And your daddy is so sweet," Caroline said.

"I think Daddy and Joey have dissected the merits of every horse on this ranch. Sometimes I wish they would find a new subject," Caleb said.

"Just be happy they like each other. We better get dressed and go for a ride before Dan and Reese get back to the bunkhouse and we get caught," Caroline said as she climbed out of bed.

Caleb watched Caroline get dressed. If he could have had his way, he would have pulled her back into bed and made love to her again. He adored the way she wasn't embarrassed to be naked in front of him. In fact, she was a bit of a flirt. She seemed to do a lot of exaggerated wiggling to get into her clothes. He let out a chortle before climbing out of bed and retrieving his trousers off the floor.

The couple rode into the foothills, enjoying the nice weather. The fall days still warmed up enough that a light jacket made for pleasant riding. They found a stallion with ten mares grazing in a meadow and watched the horses from a ridge. The mustangs in the higher elevations were starting to get their winter coats due to the colder nights. Three of the older mares had begun to show they were carrying foals.

"Looks like there'll be some babies in the spring," Caroline said.

"That it does," Caleb said before pointing toward a mare. "That chestnut over there is one of them we bred to Leif. I'm anxious to see what he produces with these mustangs."

"So, Mr. Gunnar, when are we going to have our first baby?" Caroline asked.

Caleb pulled his head back and looked at her quizzically. "I don't know. I guess when the Good Lord puts in an order for us," he said.

"How many orders would you like, all told?" she asked.

Tipping his hat back, Caleb let out a sigh. "You're asking some tough questions today. I think I'll defer to the lady as to the number. After all, you'll be the one doing most of the raising of them."

"Caleb Gunnar, don't think for a minute that you're getting out of helping with children. I won't stand for that. I know I won't be able to work on the ranch as much, but I still intend to help some of the time," Caroline said.

With an impish smile, Caleb said, "We'll just dump them with Claire. It'll give her something to do. And I bet Joey will be plumb silly over them."

Caroline let out a giggle. "You are terrible. Mother might not think you're such a prize if she heard such talk from you. I may use that against you, to tarnish you a little."

"She won't believe you," Caleb said.

"Do you think all the bad times are over?" she asked.

Caleb studied his bride-to-be for a moment. He had an urge to tell her what she wanted to hear but couldn't bring himself to do it. "Caroline, life always has challenges, even in the best of times—it's just the way it is. It's how we respond to the bad days that matters."

"I suppose, but it sure would be nice if it were otherwise."

"Makes you appreciate me more this way," Caleb said as he nudged his horse. "Let's ride. You're talking too much."

By the time Caleb and Caroline got back to the ranch after their ride, the others had made it back from town. Dusk began settling over the landscape as the horses were put in their stalls and fed. The young couple slipped into the kitchen and made boiled pork sandwiches. Neither had eaten since breakfast. They tore off chunks of meat in a manner that would have received a rebuke from either of their mothers.

Afterward, they joined Joey and their parents in the parlor for games of charades. Claire kept everyone's glass topped up with brandy, so as the evening wore on, the games became louder and more animated. Even Olivia joined the other two women in fits of giggles. Nils sat in his chair with a bemused smile as if the whole world seemed funny. By the time the games ended, Caroline was walking with a slight wobble. She kissed Caleb goodnight and disappeared to her room. Joey and Caleb said their goodbyes and headed toward the bunkhouse.

"That must have been some ride you took today," Joey said.

"I guess so," Caleb said, not sure where the conversation was headed.

"I just bet you did," Joey said.

"What's that supposed to mean?" Caleb asked.

"Oh stop being so sly. You didn't fool Claire or me, and I doubt you fooled your parents. We knew what you two were up to. You and Caroline are like a couple of kids sneaking around," Joey said.

"You've just forgotten what it's like to be young."

Joey let out a little guffaw. "I ain't that old. I know I'm not going to miss this old bunkhouse. The only downside I see to moving into Claire's house is that you're coming, too. I'm not sure how well two sets of newlyweds are going to work out around here."

Both men started to laugh. Though they'd known each other less than a year, their bond had been forged in adversity. It ran as deep as the most loyal of families. Caleb considered Joey to be the best friend he'd ever had.

"There might be a lot of retiring for naps," Caleb joked as they entered the building.

Dan and Reese sat at the table playing dominoes. They gave the men a lukewarm greeting. They were trying to be good sports about all the changes about to happen at the ranch, but the weddings were weighing heavily on their minds. The knowledge that the ranch foreman was marrying one of the ranch's owners and a ranch hand was marrying the other had caused Lucky Shoat to quit a couple of weeks ago. As Lucky had cleaned out his belongings he had said, "There's going to be an awful lot of chiefs around here, and not many Indians."

Caleb and Joey, sensing that the men felt left out, sat down and joined the game. They played past midnight. When there was more yawning going on than playing, the men decided to turn in for the night.

Chapter 4

The mountains near Empire City, Colorado

September 08, 1877

Levi just wanted to be alone after spending a few days dealing with the Shumans. He wished they would head out for a robbery or just go to town to raise some hell. Since they still had plenty of money from their last heist, they seemed to be content to sit around as long as the whiskey held out. Ellis was the only one who would speak to him, but only when absolutely necessary. All the tension and keeping his guard up wore on Levi. He didn't like to be left alone with Bluebird, but he was so sick of listening to the drunken rants of the Shumans that he would have gladly endured the Indian's silence. Truth be told, Bluebird put more fear into him than the three Shumans combined. He tried avoiding her as much as possible, but sometimes he would catch her staring at him with those piercing brown eyes. She wouldn't even bother to look away when he caught her. Their exchanges made him wonder what she was thinking. Sometimes it sent a shiver down his spine. He knew an Indian could slit a man's throat without making a sound.

The Shumans stayed up most of the night whooping and a hollering and making it nearly impossible for him to sleep. Levi came to the conclusion that the men weren't leaving anytime soon. Needing money anyway, he decided to ride out again. This time, he was determined to stick to his plan of robbing settlers.

Levi fixed himself a big breakfast in the morning and left the hideout as soon as he finished his meal. As he traveled, he found the silence he'd been seeking drowned out by his own overactive mind. He pondered how he ever let himself fall to such a lowly existence. After running away from his uncle, he'd tried to find work—but with no success, he got hungry. In desperation, he had robbed an old drunk one night outside a saloon. From that point on, the notion of looking for honest work never again occurred to him. Now, eleven years later, he didn't have much more to show for his efforts than he had on the night he committed his first crime. Levi put his horse into a lope and tried not to think.

When he reached Idaho Springs, he detoured down side streets and slunk through the town. He tried to look straight ahead, but caught himself casting furtive glances around for any sign of the miners who had been in the trading post during his botched robbery attempt. Nobody seemed to be paying him any mind. Once he made it past the town, he took off at a trot until he'd covered a few miles.

Two days later, Levi reached a spot on the plains where he'd had luck in the past finding settlers headed to start their new lives in either Denver or the goldfields. He made camp in a grove of cottonwoods along a creek and watched the horizon. Toward sunset, a single covered wagon stopped about a quarter of a mile upstream. Levi preferred the settlers to be in the midst of setting up camp before he rode in. That way, he could be sure no one was lurking in the back of the wagon—a lesson he had learned by almost getting his head blown off once. He waited a half hour before saddling his horse.

A woman was scooping some lard into a frying pan as Levi entered the camp. A man and a boy were stacking firewood. None of them saw him until his horse nickered. The settlers looked up in surprise at the Colt revolver pointed at them.

"I don't want to hurt anybody. Just give me your money, watches, and jewelry, and I'll be on my way," Levi said as he climbed down from his horse. He didn't wear a mask—he only bothered to tuck his long hair into his hat.

"We don't have much. You're going to leave us without money for supplies. We're poor folks," the man said.

"Anything is better than nothing," Levi replied.

A little girl of about four years of age emerged from behind the wagon. Surprised, Levi pointed his gun at the child. She smiled at him. In her hands were wildflowers that she had picked.

The woman let out a wail. "Don't shoot my baby," she cried.

"Ma'am, I'm not going to harm a child," Levi said as he trained the gun back at the man.

"Jeanie, come here right this minute," the mother ordered.

Jeanie smiled at Levi again and began walking toward him.

"Come here, right now," the mother yelled. She started to move toward her daughter, but froze in her tracks for fear of getting shot.

The little girl strolled up to Levi and offered him the flowers. Some long-lost memory stirred in Levi. He couldn't quite remember the details, but he knew it had something to do with him bringing his momma a bouquet of blue scorpion weed. His eyes got misty, and he had to set his jaw to control his emotions as he took the flowers from Jeanie.

Levi patted the child on the head. "Thank you, honey. I reckon flowers are enough loot for one day. Sorry to have bothered you folks."

He climbed back on his horse and took off in a gallop, following the creek. As he rode, Levi started crying like a baby. He couldn't help himself. The tears blurred his vision to the point where he could barely see. Glancing down, he noticed he still held the flowers in a death grip. The memory came flooding back. His momma had taken the flowers he'd offered and told him they made the most beautiful bouquet she'd ever seen. She had put them in a glass vase and placed it on the kitchen table. The recollection caused Levi to swear aloud that his life of crime was over with for good. He would never bring shame to his mother's memory again.

Levi ran his horse until a lather covered its shiny coat. He slowed the animal to a walk to cool it down, satisfied that several miles separated him from the settlers. He made camp along the creek and pondered what he wanted to do next with his life. He decided he needed a change of scenery for his new start. He would head north. With the fire dying, he crawled into his bedroll with the intention of returning to the hideout to retrieve his few meager possessions before setting out on a new course. That night, he dreamed of his family in vivid details of happy times in their home. That hadn't happened in years.

On each day of travel back to the hideout, Levi felt a little better about himself. He realized that he didn't have many skills for landing a job, but he did know a little blacksmithing and he was a pretty good horseman. With a little luck, he figured he could find a job as a cowboy on a cattle ranch somewhere.

When Levi rode into the hideout, he thought it seemed a little too quiet. He looked around and noticed two horses were missing from the grazing area. Bluebird stood in the yard, boiling something in a pot that stunk. He could feel her stare as he rode past her.

Ellis poked his head out the door with his rifle ready. "Oh it's you," he muttered.

"Where are Harper and Jordan?" Levi asked as he climbed off his horse.

"They headed to town this morning to get a bad itch scratched," Ellis said. He laughed as if he'd made the funniest statement on record. "They might be gone a day or two."

"I came back to get my belongings. I'm headed out for greener pastures," Levi said.

"Can't say we're going to miss you," Ellis said with a slight edge to his voice.

"Those two half-witted cousins of yours will get you killed one of these days," Levi said. He untied his saddlebags and carried them past Ellis and into the cabin.

Levi pulled out a box he kept under his bunk. In it he had two changes of clothes, his old copy of *David Copperfield*, and a couple of other books he'd bought over the years. He picked up *David Copperfield* and flipped through the dog-eared pages. The book still made him nostalgic for the days when he'd believed he could persevere through living with his uncle to become a lawyer. He realized now that the idea had always been a lark, but dreams died hard.

The wilted flowers from the little girl were stashed in Levi's saddlebag. He retrieved them and carefully placed them between the pages of the book to serve as a reminder of his vow to change his life.

From out in the yard, he heard Ellis yelling. Then Bluebird screamed.

Levi let out a sigh and rubbed the back of his neck. He contemplated whether beginning a new life required always doing the right thing. He knew his feelings about Indians hadn't changed, but he stood and walked out onto the porch reluctantly.

Bluebird was curled up in a ball on the ground. Ellis kept booting her in the ass, trying to get her to move.

"Ellis, leave Bluebird alone," Levi warned.

Ellis spun in Levi's direction. "This ain't none of your concern. Since when do you care how I treat my squaw?"

"Looks like I started today," Levi said.

Swinging his leg again, Ellis gave Bluebird another good kick and then glared at Levi with a sneer on his face.

In a voice that was calm but forceful, Levi said, "This is your last warning. Leave her alone."

"I don't know why we didn't kill you a long time ago. Harper is right. You do think you're better than us," Ellis said.

Ellis went for his gun. Levi drew his Colt and fired two shots before the outlaw had leveled his weapon. The shots thudded into Ellis's chest, driving him backward. He spilled the pot Bluebird had been tending to, before collapsing onto the ground. Levi glanced at his gun as if it had acted on its own accord. Things had happened so fast that there hadn't been time to think, only react. He walked over to Ellis. The outlaw had the unmistakable look of the dead, with opened eyes gazing into the heavens. Levi had to will himself not to puke in front of Bluebird. His stomach seemed as if it was doing somersaults, and he felt flush. He holstered his revolver and glanced down at the Indian to avoid having to look at the dead man again.

Bluebird stood up and brushed the dirt off her buckskins. Her facial expression gave away absolutely no hint of whatever she thought or felt. Once she had cleaned herself to her satisfaction, she looked Levi in the eyes as if she was waiting for him to speak.

Levi had a hard time meeting Bluebird's gaze. She made him incredibly uncomfortable. He almost feared she had some mystical powers, though he had to admit to himself that she probably wouldn't be in such a dire situation if she did.

"You can stay here and put up with Harper and Jordan if you want. They may think you killed Ellis, and you know they will want to share you. Or you can take Ellis's horse and be free."

Bluebird nodded her head before scampering into the cabin to retrieve some food, what few clothes she owned, and anything else she deemed worth taking. Levi saddled Ellis's horse for her before he went inside to finish gathering his own belongings. They left the hideout together without Levi saying another word to the Indian.

As they weaved their way down the narrow trail, Levi couldn't stop thinking about the murder he'd just committed. He knew the Shumans had always been leery of his skills with a firearm. He'd really thought that Ellis would back down when he'd ordered him to stop beating Bluebird.

The irony was not lost on him that the first thing he had accomplished after deciding to straighten out his life was to shoot a man to death. He hoped he never had to kill again. He figured he needed to cover a lot of territory, for as sure as his name was Levi Bolander, Harper and Jordan would come looking for him.

Once Levi and Bluebird reached the main trail, Levi turned east toward Denver. He kept expecting Bluebird to head south down a mountain pass in the direction of New Mexico, but she continued riding along with him. Levi knew Indians were skilled at navigation, so he felt certain Bluebird wasn't confused about what direction they were traveling or how to get home. He didn't say anything for a time. He just kept on riding, anticipating she would leave eventually.

Another hour passed, and Bluebird was still riding with him. He stopped his horse and pointed at the sun. "Bluebird, I'm going to be heading north into the Wyoming Territory. You need to go south to get back to the New Mexico Territory."

"I go with you," Bluebird said.

Levi pulled his head back as if hearing a voice from a ghost. Finding out that Bluebird wasn't a mute—and that she could speak English—proved even more of a shock than the words she had spoken. He wouldn't have been any more flabbergasted if a dog had talked. "You need to go find your family."

"Family all dead," she said.

"Listen, Bluebird, I'm done robbing people. I'm going to get a job. I can't take care of you, and you don't owe me anything," Levi said.

"Nowhere to go. I go with you," Bluebird repeated.

Levi let out a sigh as he wondered if trying to live right was going to be more dangerous than being an outlaw. Second thoughts about his decision to rescue Bluebird from the beating crept into his mind. She didn't seem willing to take no for an answer, and he no longer had the will to be mean enough to make her leave. As he looked at Bluebird, he wondered what went on inside her head and why she wanted to be with him. He had ignored her the whole time they had known each other. He sighed again, knowing he was stuck with an Indian who he didn't truly trust. For all he knew, she could be related to the very people who had killed his family.

"Let's get to riding then. We got about an hour of light left," Levi said as he nudged his horse in the ribs.

Chapter 5

The plains east of Fort Collins, Colorado

September 13, 1877

Levi and Bluebird had put in some hard traveling, managing to make it through the mountains and past Denver on their northward trek. Levi had contemplated abandoning her as they passed through the town, but never really came up with a plan that he thought would succeed. His conscience got the better of him every time he thought about doing it. He just didn't see how he could keep his vow to become a person his mother would have been proud of if he mistreated Bluebird— even though he still didn't have a clue with what to do with the Indian. Every time he broached the subject, Bluebird's steadfast answer remained, "I go with you."

Worrying that the Shumans would catch them led Levi to look over his shoulder constantly and to sleep poorly at night. Bluebird seemed to have no concerns about the matter, and she would slow their pace by stopping to pick or pull plants that caught her fancy. She would shove them into her saddlebag or a pouch she wore around her neck. In the evenings, she tended to the plants, drying some, crushing leaves on a few, and keeping only the roots of others. At first, Levi feared

Bluebird might be making a poison with which to kill him before deciding the idea made no sense. For whatever reason, she wanted to be with him.

Bluebird climbed off her horse again and began picking wildflowers. She never bothered to give Levi a warning when she was about to stop for some plant that garnered her interest. He had ridden on a couple of times with the hope she might not follow, but she always returned to his side a few minutes later.

"Harper and Jordan are going to find us if you keep poking along," Levi warned.

"I need to make medicines," Bluebird replied.

"You need to hurry," Levi said.

"I not worried about those ... idiots," she said, smiling with pride at her new word.

"I'm," Levi corrected. "You might change your mind if they catch us."

In spite of his loathing of Indians, Levi found himself talking to Bluebird constantly to pass the time. He'd even gotten into the habit of helping her with English. With each passing day, she contributed more to the conversation.

"I'll let you know if they coming," she said.

"What makes you think you'll know before I do?" Levi asked, irritated by the perceived slight.

Bluebird smiled but did not answer the question. She grabbed two more handfuls of goldenrod and quickly shoved them into her saddlebag before climbing back onto her horse.

"Let's quit talking and go," she said with a grin.

They rode for the rest of the day and made camp beside a stream. Each night Levi depended on finding wild game to shoot for them to have something to eat.

He was nearly out of money, and supplies were running low. In Denver, he had only bought hardtack and cartridges. He grabbed his rifle and took off into the brush. After hunting for over an hour, he gave up on finding anything to shoot. He walked back toward camp, dejected that the meal for the night would be hardtack. As he got closer, he imagined he caught a whiff of something cooking. A few steps later, he recognized the unmistakable smell of fish frying. Back at the camp, he found Bluebird hunched over his frying pan, tending to a meal.

"How did you catch those?" Levi asked.

Bluebird picked up some twine with attached bone hooks and held them for Levi to see. "I carry." She said.

"What did you use for bait?" he wanted to know.

She looked at him a moment with one eye squinted and her mouth set tightly shut as she tried to decipher the question. A look of revelation came over her, and she showed him where she had pulled up clumps of weeds. She pointed at a bug.

"Grubs," Levi said.

"Grubs," Bluebird repeated.

Levi smiled. "Well, aren't you resourceful? This sure beats hardtack, Bluebird," he said.

Bluebird smiled back. "Sit. Fish ready."

As they were eating, Levi said, "We need supplies, but I'm about out of money. I don't know what we're going to do. No cattle ranch is going to hire me with you tagging along, and I can't afford a room to get a job in town."

Bluebird reached over into her saddlebag and retrieved a leather pouch that jingled as she handed it to Levi. The weight of the contents surprised him as he bounced the bag in his palm. He opened it and poured twenty-dollar gold pieces into his hand until they spilled over and started to fall to the ground. Counting quickly, Levi tallied twenty-six coins.

Looking up in astonishment, he asked, "Where did you get these?"

"I'm Ellis squaw. He dead. They mine now," Bluebird answered.

The color drained from Levi's face. He rubbed the back of his neck. "Jordan and Harper are coming for us as sure as I'm sitting here. Those two don't really scare me, but if they surprise us or catch us out in the middle of nowhere, well, then I don't like our odds," he said.

Bluebird leaned over and patted Levi's leg. It was the first time they had ever touched. "We be okay. I watch for them," she said.

"No, it is not okay," Levi yelled. His face turned red, and he rubbed his neck again. "Indians killed my family. I don't like you and I don't know why you are here. I'm trying to start a new life, but here I am—stuck with you."

Though she tried to put on a stoic face, Levi could see he had hurt Bluebird's feelings badly. He didn't care. All he wanted to do was settle down and get a job. He didn't see how that would be possible with Bluebird with him. He attempted to give her the pouch of coins, but she pushed his hand away.

"Money yours now. You buy us supplies," she said.

"The money is yours," Levi said as he tried again to hand her the bag.

In a defiant voice, Bluebird shouted, "No."

Her dark eyes seemed to bore right through him as she gave him a hard stare. He wanted to look away, but forced himself to meet her gaze head-on. As the battle of wills played out, Levi wished he could feel hate for the Indian woman so that he could justify leaving her, but his anger was fading and he couldn't summon the emotion. He dropped the pouch by his foot.

"We better get to eating before our food gets cold," he said to end the standoff.

They ate their meal in silence. Levi wouldn't look at Bluebird, but he could sense her eyes upon him. He began feeling bad for yelling at her. He wondered if Indians had the same emotions as white people. In the past, he'd always thought of them as savages no more capable of feelings than a mad dog, but Bluebird didn't seem much different from any other woman he'd known. The idea that she probably felt things the same way a white woman would was a revelation for him. He looked up from his plate.

"The fish tasted very good. Thank you."

"You welcome."

The compliment flattered her. Her eyes lit up, and the corners of her mouth formed an ever-so-slight smile.

"You are welcome," Levi corrected.

"You are welcome," Bluebird repeated.

Levi let out a little laugh. "Oh Lordy, what have I gotten myself into this time?" he asked rhetorically.

Chapter 6

Langley Ranch, Wyoming Territory

September 14, 1877

As morning's first gray light appeared through the bunkhouse window, Caleb awoke. Joey usually cooked breakfast, so Caleb quietly headed to the barn to feed the horses. He hoped that a hot plate of eggs and bacon would be waiting upon his return. He fed Diablo, the gelding that he rode on most days, and then Buddy, Caroline's favorite. It wasn't until he moved to Leif's stall that he realized the stallion was gone. Caleb panicked for a moment before deciding his daddy had probably taken his long-prized horse for a ride. He finished feeding the other animals, then walked out of the barn. In the pale light, he could just recognize his father sitting on the porch, smoking his pipe.

"Daddy, did you move Leif?" Caleb called out.

Nils stood and began walking toward his son. "I just got up and came outside for a smoke. Where would he be?"

The hairs on Caleb's neck stood on end, and he could feel a knot forming in his empty stomach. "I'm going to rouse the bunkhouse. You had better get the ladies out of bed. I'm afraid he might have been stolen. His stall door was latched—he sure didn't close it on the way out."

By the time everyone had gathered in the barnyard, the morning had lightened enough that they could see well. Caleb and Joey walked around the barn, finding the telltale signs of two sets of boot prints leading Leif away.

"He's been stolen," Caleb said as he returned to the group.

"I don't see how. Nobody even knew we had him. You've never ridden him anywhere that people could see him," Caroline said as she rubbed her forehead.

"Daddy, did you tell anyone about Leif?" Caleb asked.

"No, of course not. We took precautions to make sure no one suspected we were headed out here. Everybody back home thinks we are at your aunt's place in Kentucky," Nils answered.

"Lucky Shoat," Reese said. "You know how he likes to run his mouth, and he didn't leave here any too happy. He's probably been in a saloon telling anyone who would listen about Leif."

Caleb let out a sigh. He decided Reese's reasoning made a lot of sense. "Do you think Lucky did it?" he asked.

"I don't think he has enough gumption to be a horse thief. He probably just talked too much," Reese replied.

"I can't believe we didn't hear anything. I would have thought Leif would've made a fuss," Caleb said.

"He knows Lucky," Joey reminded him.

Silence fell over the group as they contemplated Joey's remark.

"I should have listened to you about getting a dog," Caroline said. She had refused to consider the idea from the start. As a child, her daddy had given her a puppy that she adored. As the dog had grown older, it had developed a taste for chickens, so her daddy had to shoot it. She'd vowed never to have another pet.

"That's water under the bridge," Caleb said.

Joey removed his hat and ran his fingers through his hair. "Caleb and I will have to track them down. There's a good chance we won't be back in time for the weddings to happen as scheduled—unless they didn't go far."

Claire looked crestfallen. Her shoulders sagged, and she tilted her head toward the ground. "You have no choice. We have to get Caleb's horse back. Everybody come in the house. I'll fix breakfast. You need to leave on a full stomach."

"I'm going with Caleb and Joey," Nils said. "That horse would have never made it into this world if I hadn't been there to pull it on the night it was born."

"Daddy, I don't know if that's a good idea. This is a harsh land," Caleb said.

"You know I can ride all day. I insist," Nils stated.

"He'll be fine. We can scrape him up some gear," Joey said to head off an argument.

By the time Claire had cooked enough eggs, biscuits, bacon, and ham for eight people, Caleb and Joey had gathered up all the supplies they would need. Their saddlebags were stuffed with cartridges, hardtack, and beef jerky. They had readied a horse for Nils with a rifle, bedroll, and a slicker.

Claire did her best to bring some levity to the meal, but failed miserably. She glanced around the table at some of the unhappiest faces she had seen in a while. Caroline looked to be on the verge of tears, and poor

Olivia seemed to be in a state of shock at her husband's plans to help find Leif. Dan and Reese ate in silence. Joey and Caleb were so lost in thought that they weren't even tasting their food.

"Maybe I should go, too," Caroline said, breaking the silence hanging over the room.

Caleb snapped out of his reverie. He looked up at Caroline. He opened his mouth to speak, but no words came.

Claire could see that her future son-in-law was struggling how to tell Caroline no without getting her daughter all worked up.

In an authoritative tone, Claire said, "Absolutely not. We have weddings in a few days, and you need to be here to help me prepare. It will give us more time to spend with Olivia, too."

With her mouth set a little too tight—a sign that revealed annoyance to those who knew her well—Caroline shot her mother a look. She knew she'd been boxed into a corner. Her mother played the wedding card, then doubled down by throwing Olivia in for good measure. All eyes in the room seemed to be boring down on her as they waited for her to speak. "You're right, Mother," she said.

Caleb glanced at Claire and tried not to smile. He felt as if one burden had been lifted. It wasn't that Caroline couldn't ride as well as the rest of them, but from past experience, he'd found that when danger appeared, his attention had been diverted toward her safety. He wouldn't have that worry now.

Once the meal was finished, Dan and Reese left to finish the chores. The others said their goodbyes.

Caroline pulled Caleb around to the side of the house. "Don't think that I don't know that Mother just did your dirty work for you. If you two start teaming up against me, I just might not think you're man enough to share my bed," she teased.

"I don't know what you're talking about," Caleb said with a grin. "But from what I've seen of you, I don't think you can keep your hands off me."

"Aren't you full of yourself?" she said.

"Just confident."

"For all I know, you hid Leif just so you could get out of marrying me," Caroline said.

"Yeah, that's it. I'd rather keep on sleeping on a cot in a room full of men than share a bed with a pretty little thing like you," Caleb said in a deadpan voice.

"Well, aren't you sweet?"

Caleb leaned down and kissed Caroline. "I love you."

"I love you, too. You be careful. I couldn't bear something happening to you," Caroline said.

"Don't you worry about that. I'll be back as soon as we can," Caleb said before giving Caroline a long goodbye kiss.

The men mounted up and followed the hoofprints to the south. Joey proved to be the best tracker of the three men, though he would have never made it as a real scout. They made good time by following the path the two riders and Leif had taken—until they encountered rocky ground. Then they began to lose minutes while they searched to pick up the trail again. The tracks led toward Fort Laramie, then veered around the town and headed in a southwesterly direction. Tracking became easier once they reached a road that the horse thieves had clearly taken.

"Where do you think they are headed?" Caleb asked.

Joey scanned the horizon before speaking. "I don't have a clue. They're following the Cheyenne and Black Hills Stage route right now."

"I know that," Caleb said a bit defensively. "I thought maybe you knew of somebody in this direction that might be interested in Leif."

"No, can't say that I do," Joey replied.

"This is certainly the way we came into Fort Laramie," Nils added.

The men continued following the well-used trail for the rest of the day. Leif had a bigger hoof than most horses, so and his prints made it easy to follow the horse thieves without getting confused by the assortment of other tracks.

"I guess they aren't stopping anywhere close," Caleb said as he glanced at the sun sinking to the west.

"No. I'm thinking they're headed to Cheyenne for the auction," Joey said.

After riding for another hour, Joey decided they should make camp along a creek for the night. He and Nils gathered firewood along the creek bank while Caleb went off in search of game.

"That's a fine son that you raised there," Joey said as he snapped a branch off a fallen tree.

"That he is. I just wish I could have taught him to harness that temper of his. He doesn't rile that easily, but when he does, he can get blind with rage. He wouldn't be a wanted man if he would have thought things through," Nils said, looking in the direction that Caleb had disappeared.

"I don't know how your daughter is doing since losing her husband, but I think that things have turned out to be a blessing for Caleb. I know killing his brother-in-law weighs heavy upon him, but it was in self-defense. He's changed so much since I've known him. He's happy and he's marrying a swell gal. I can surely say I know both of them well. Believe me, they bring out the best in each other," Joey said.

"You may have a point. I never looked at it that way before now. And I can see that Caleb is back to being his old self. There were times after his wife and baby died that I thought he might die too from the grief. His sister, Britt, has moved on and is making a new life for herself. She's better off without Charles. It might not be my place to say, but if any human deserved to die, it certainly was him. He was a bane for the human race," Nils said before dropping an armload of wood onto the ground.

The sound of a rifle carried over from the other side of some hills.

"Let's hope he didn't miss, or we'll be eating jerky tonight," Joey said as he dropped his load of branches onto the pile.

Joey pulled some dead grass and wadded it up into a ball before grabbing some of the smaller sticks and arranging them on top of the straw. With a strike of the match, the grass caught fire and soon ignited the sticks. By the time Caleb returned to camp carrying a jackrabbit, Joey had the campfire blazing.

"That's the biggest rabbit I've ever seen in my life. We won't go hungry tonight," Nils said.

"They grow them big out here, Daddy. This is a jackrabbit," Caleb informed him.

"Let me skin it. I want to get my hands on that thing," Nils said.

Caleb handed him the rabbit. "You won't get any argument from me."

Dusk had settled in by the time Nils finished cleaning the game. Caleb hung the meat from the spit he'd fashioned and took a seat beside his father to watch the rabbit roast.

"Now that we're clear of all the womenfolk, tell me more about Caroline," Nils said.

Caleb let out a chuckle. "We certainly didn't hit it off. In fact, the only reason that I took the ranch hand job there was because she insulted us Southerners. She challenged me to ride that horse right there," he said, pointing toward Diablo. "I told her that if I could ride him, she'd have to pay me ten dollars a month over the other ranch hands. Nobody had ever been able to stay on Diablo. I don't think I've ever seen a horse more scared of humans, but I calmed him down. He never even bucked. After that, I tried to be a burr under her saddle. She was a pain in my backside. I guess all the troubles we had with the mustangs getting shot—and me telling her about killing Charles—kind of changed things."

Joey laughed and slapped his leg. "That's Caleb's story. I knew before the first week was over where they were headed. I just had to keep them from killing each other until they figured things out for themselves. They were so scared of what they felt that they did their best to drive each other away."

"So he says. I think there's some revisionist history in that story," Caleb said.

Nils smiled at the two men. He enjoyed seeing their camaraderie. Caleb never had many close friends in his life, so his father was pleased to see he had such a loyal one now. "Caroline seems like a fine girl. It's good to see you laugh again. Your sister is much happier these days, too."

"Momma told me that Britt was more content than she had seen her in long time. I've spent a lot of nights worrying about her and what I did to her life," Caleb said.

"That's all in the past. Life goes on. Britt's a strong woman. I hope she finds herself another man someday. One that deserves her," Nils said.

The rabbit had browned, and sizzled on the stick. Caleb pulled off chunks of meat and quickly tossed them onto the plates. The conversation died as the men, starving from the day of riding, feasted on their meal. Between the three of them, they managed to eat the whole rabbit.

"That's the best rabbit I've ever had in my life," Nils said before licking his fingers.

"You're not used to skipping lunch. A hard day will make most anything taste good," Caleb said.

Turning serious, Nils asked, "Do you think we'll ever find Leif?"

Joey tossed a bone into the fire. "I was just thinking about that. I think in the morning we should quit worrying about tracking and push on toward Cheyenne. We can ask anybody we come across if they've seen two riders with a stallion. Otherwise, I fear we will never catch them."

"Sounds good to me," Caleb said.

Nils nodded his head.

The men talked for a little while longer, then weariness set in and they crawled into their bedrolls for the night.

At the first sign of light the next morning, Nils arose. He felt cold and moved stiffly. Grabbing a stick, he began stirring the coals. He threw some branches onto the remnants of the campfire. The wood ignited, and Nils leaned over the flames to warm himself.

Caleb and Joey stirred in their bedrolls.

"It's a wonder to me how the temperature drops so much out here and then warms right back up the next day," Nils said.

As Joey climbed out of his bedroll, he said, "The weather does take some getting used to. It certainly is different from where I'm from in Illinois, or your Tennessee. Your son is going to gain a whole new appreciation for cold when winter sets in."

"That's why I'm marrying the boss—so I can stay in bed and let the others work out in it," Caleb joked.

The men ate a breakfast of beef jerky and hardtack. They were back in the saddle by the time there was enough morning light to see well. They traveled at a walk until the horses warmed up their muscles, then put their mounts into a lope.

They had traveled for just over an hour when up ahead in the distance they could see two riders kicking up dust as they rode hard toward them. Joey pulled his spyglass from his saddlebag and studied the men.

"Those men are in an awfully big hurry for so early in the morning. Their horses already look to be about tuckered out," Joey said as continued looking through his spyglass.

"I wonder if they're being chased," Caleb mused.

"That's what I'm thinking. It's not like there's anything around here to be in such an all-fire hurry to get to," Joey said.

"Daddy, maybe you should ride off to the side—in case there's trouble," Caleb suggested.

"Nonsense," Nils replied. He pulled his rifle from its scabbard and rested the gun across the saddle and his thighs.

Caleb and Joey looked at each other, and Joey gave a quick nod of his head. They retrieved their rifles. Hoping that the riders would pass without trouble, all three men moved their horses to the side of the trail and separated so as not to be clustered together.

As the riders got to within a hundred yards, they drew their revolvers and continued riding at a gallop.

"I'm afraid they plan to try to kill us to get our horses. Let's hold our fire until we know. We don't want to kill somebody by mistake," Joey said.

The two riders continued charging, their horses covered in foam and their tongues drooping from their mouths. One of the horses stumbled, nearly throwing the man. A moment later, the riders raised their pistols and fired. Caleb and Joey had fought in the War Between the States. They had learned long ago to stay calm in the heat of battle. Nils had a reputation back in Tennessee as being one of the best shots in Chalksville. They raised their rifles as the riders fired a second round at them. The countryside exploded with noise as the three men sent a barrage of shots at the advancing men. One horse and rider crashed to the ground. The second rider was knocked off the back of his horse. As soon as the riderless horse came to a halt, silence returned to the countryside as quickly as it had been interrupted.

"Is anybody hit?" Caleb asked as he nervously looked toward his daddy and Joey.

"I'm fine," Joey answered.

"Me too," Nils replied.

Caleb could see the rifle in his father's hands trembling. His daddy was so shaken that he had trouble dismounting.

"Be careful," Joey warned as they walked toward the bodies.

The rider on the downed horse had bullets in his head, neck, and chest. He had no doubt been dead by the time he hit the ground. The horse had taken a bullet to the head; it kicked its legs a couple of times before succumbing to the injury. The second rider was drenched in blood from bullet wounds to the chest and shoulder. He writhed on the ground and began moaning.

"What do we do now?" Caleb asked.

"Well, I half expect somebody to be coming along shortly, chasing these two. If not, we'll have to throw him over that poor horse and take him to Bordeaux. It's not very far from here," Joey answered.

"Don't you think that will kill him?" Nils inquired.

"To be honest, I don't much care. I'm funny that way when it comes to people who've tried to kill me," Joey said.

"I suppose you have a point. This surely is a wild land. I'll take his horse and ours to that creek over there to water them," Nils said as he walked off.

"I'll see if I can stop the bleeding," Caleb said.

The wounded man seemed semiconscious. He only moaned when Caleb asked questions. A bullet had hit the shoulder socket, and the man's arm hung precariously to the side. The wound to the chest spurted blood with each breath. Caleb had witnessed more than his fair share of carnage during the war. He felt certain the man was as good as dead. He shoved a bandana into the chest wound to slow the bleeding, causing the man to groan. When Nils returned with the horses, Caleb grabbed a canteen. He tipped the man's head up and managed to get some water down his throat.

The men stood around waiting to see if a posse would come. Before long, two riders approached from the south. They had their horses in a trot and made a point of keeping their hands in view. The men looked more like trappers than lawmen. To be cautious, Caleb and Joey flipped the thongs off the hammers of their revolvers.

"We heard all the gunfire. Sounded like a war. Looks like you did our dirty work for us. Hector Wiley and Truman Cash robbed my trading post first thing this morning," one of the men announced as he surveyed his surroundings.

"We killed one of them, and I fear the other one isn't going to make it. They fired upon us first," Caleb said.

"I don't doubt that. I imagine they had their eyes on some fresh horses. The darn fools were riding those animals like they were in a race. We were going at an easy pace to catch them. There weren't no way their poor old mounts were going to be able to keep going for long," the man said.

"We haven't checked their saddlebags or anything," Joey said.

"If you boys want to be on your way, we'll take it from here. I'm sorry you had to get involved with this, but I sure do appreciate it."

"We're after some people, too. Have you come across two riders with the finest-looking stallion you ever laid eyes upon? He's a dark bay, stands about fifteen and a half hands," Caleb said.

"Yes, I have. They stopped by yesterday evening and bought a few supplies. I wish I'd known. I'd gladly have returned the favor. The more of these varmints we put in the grave, the better off this country will be. I mentioned what a fine horse they had, and one of them let slip they were taking him to the auction in Cheyenne. I guess I should have figured something was up when the other one gave him a dirty look," the man said.

"Much obliged," Caleb said.

"No, much obliged to you. I hope you get your horse back and serve some justice."

"Let's get going," Joey said, anxious to get back on the trail.

The men rode away. They hadn't traveled more than a couple hundred yards when they heard a single shot behind them.

"They put him out of his misery. I don't think I could ever do such a thing," Caleb said.

"That they did. I couldn't do it either," Joey said. "Let's see if we can make up some time."

Nils looked over at Caleb and Joey. His face betrayed shock and dismay. "What kind of place is this, where a man kills another like a horse with a ruined leg?"

"Nils, that's the first time in my life that I've witnessed that happening. I thought they'd at least throw him over a horse and take him back to the trading post. I don't think he would have made it there alive either way, but you are right—that's a cold-blooded thing to do," Joey said.

"Speaking of first times, that's the first time in my life that I've been shot at—and the first time I've ever shot at someone," Nils said as the enormity of what had just transpired slowly settled into his consciousness.

"Daddy, things are different out here. Law and order haven't really gotten this far west. A man has to protect himself and what's his. It's just the way it is," Caleb said.

"We'll never speak a word of this to your momma," Nils said, ending the conversation.

Chapter 7

Near Cheyenne, Wyoming

September 16, 1877

Cheyenne turned out to be a bust. Levi had ridden into the town determined to find a job. With Bluebird's money, he'd figured they could get a room at hotel. He quickly learned that nobody was interested in hiring a drifter who had just showed up in their fine city. Dejected, he bought supplies and then they headed on to the north. He didn't know what else to do but put more distance between themselves and the Shumans.

Bluebird, sensing Levi's frustration, rode along in silence. She feared any conversation from her would unleash his anger over the fact she wouldn't leave. Truth be told, she felt frustrated, too. She certainly never wanted to be kidnapped or to live in some hideout away from anybody she'd ever known. And now she had no idea where any of her people were or how to find them. Back when she was Ellis's squaw, she'd known that Levi was the only one of the bunch with any honor and had wondered how he'd stood by and watched her be mistreated. Sticking with him now seemed like her only option. She liked Levi, but harbored some resentment that he hadn't come to her rescue a long time before he did.

They set up camp along a creek, and Levi took off in search of game. By the time he returned with a jackrabbit, Bluebird had the fire burning hot. She made a spit while Levi cleaned the rabbit. Neither was in the mood for conversation, so they ate the meal in silence. Afterward, Bluebird went off in search of plants in the last light of evening, leaving Levi to mull their options.

When Bluebird walked back into camp, Levi said, "I guess we'll just keep riding and hope we have better luck in the next town we come to. We'll be that much farther from the Shumans anyway."

"I'm sorry to be . . . trouble. I don't know where to go," Bluebird said.

Levi let out a sigh. "I know. We'll figure something out eventually."

Seeing Levi's improved mood, curiosity got the better of Bluebird. "Why did you help me that day?"

Looking up, Levi studied Bluebird's face for a moment. Shame came over him for having waited so long to rescue her. He tried to think of how to explain himself so that she could understand. "I was a bad man, but I don't want to be bad anymore. I needed to start doing what was right."

"You want to be honor?" Bluebird asked.

"Honorable. Yes, I do," he said.

Bluebird smiled sadly and nodded her head. She felt she now understood her traveling partner a little better. She banished her resentment that he had never helped her sooner. She'd seen men fall many times and had come to know it was the standing back up that mattered.

Levi returned the smile. For the first time since they left the hideout, he didn't look at her as an obligation. He felt some compassion stirring for his traveling companion. He'd spent so much time with Bluebird in the last few days that he'd slowly stopped thinking of her as an Indian and begun to view her as he would any woman.

"When I would catch you staring at me at the hideout, what were you thinking?" Levi asked.

Pausing for a moment as she chose her words, Bluebird said, "I see lost man want to be honorable. I wonder when he come."

With a sigh, Levi said, "I guess late is better than never. I'm sure going to try not to lose that man again."

"You strong now. You be fine," Bluebird assured Levi.

They turned in for the night as soon as it grew dark, with the plan to hit the trail early the next morning.

The smell of breakfast cooking woke Levi from his sleep. He opened his eyes to see that the sun had already risen. Glancing toward the fire, he saw Bluebird tending to a skillet of the salt pork he'd purchased in Cheyenne. She hummed an Indian melody and didn't notice him watching her.

"Smells good," Levi said.

Bluebird jumped at the sound of Levi's voice, then smiled. "Get up. Food ready," she said.

She retrieved their tin plates and forked the meat onto them as Levi took a seat by the fire.

"I think today is going to be better than yesterday," Levi said as he cut a bite of pork.

"You find job," Bluebird said.

"I hope so. This pork is pretty tasty," he said.

"Pork pretty?" she asked.

Levi let out a laugh. "Pork tastes good," he said.

"Oh," Bluebird replied, still confused.

After scarfing down the meal, Levi needed to relieve himself. He was extremely self-conscious about such matters, so he took off into some bushes along a rock ridge. As he buttoned up his pants, he looked over his shoulder to make sure that Bluebird wasn't anywhere in sight. He took a step and felt his foot come down on something soft. An instant later, a rattlesnake that had been sunning itself on the rocks sank its fangs into his calf just above his boot. Levi let out a yell as the snake slithered away.

"A rattler bit me," Levi hollered as he walked into camp.

Bluebird jumped up and ran to Levi.

"Lie down," she said as she grabbed his hand and pulled him toward his bedroll.

Levi did as he was told. Bluebird yanked his boot off, then grabbed his knife from the sheath he wore on his belt. She slit his trousers up past the knee to get her first look at the wound. The punctures were deep into his muscles. She hustled to her saddlebag to retrieve a plant that the Indians called "white man's footprint" and shoved the leaves into her mouth. After chewing the plant into a paste, she applied it to the wounds.

"Stay still," Bluebird warned to stop Levi continually bending his injured leg.

"I'm sorry," Levi said.

"Eat this," she said, holding out more of the plant.

"I'm not eating that," he said.

"Eat it," Bluebird demanded in a voice filled with authority.

Levi warily took the plant and began chewing the leaves. Each time he swallowed, he made a face.

"Am I going to die?" Levi asked.

"No, I heal you. I go find more plant," Bluebird said before scurrying off into the grassland.

Bluebird returned carrying several more white man's footprint plants that she had picked. She insisted Levi eat some more leaves. The wounds already looked inflamed, and his leg had begun to swell. An hour later, he was moaning from the pain of the bite. His face was covered in perspiration. He rolled onto his side and vomited. Bluebird chewed up some more leaves and applied a fresh poultice. She then retrieved one of Levi's shirts, dunked it into the creek, and wrapped it around his head.

∞

Lucky Shoat and Everett Clancy had covered a lot of territory since stopping at the trading post in Bordeaux. Everett had insisted that they put as much daylight between themselves and Fort Laramie as possible. He was a nervous wreck over stealing Leif and talked constantly of his fear of hanging.

"I think we should stop here," Lucky said as he slowed his horse.

"What? We're just a few miles from Cheyenne. Aren't we going to go on into town?" Everett asked.

"The auction isn't until tomorrow. We're going to lay low. We'll ride straight to the auction, sell that horse, and be on our way," Lucky said.

"Then why didn't we wait another day to steal it?" Everett inquired.

"Because you would have lost your nerve if we waited. I wasn't about to give you the chance to sober up. That looks like a creek over by those trees," Lucky said as he pointed at the tree line a hundred yards away. "We can make camp there. Leif will bring more money if we let him rest and get some water in him. We've done a lot of riding."

"And somebody from the Langley ranch just might catch us. We should have ridden farther on the night we stole that horse," Everett warned.

"Joey and Caleb wouldn't even find their way back to the ranch house if they didn't have those two women waiting there to pleasure them. I doubt they even went the right direction. I've let you push us too hard as it is. Just shut up and relax. Come on," Lucky said.

The two men rode to the creek, then followed the stream around a tree-lined bend with the intent of getting out of view of the trail. As they rounded the curve, they saw Levi stretched out on the ground.

"What the . . ." Lucky said as kicked his horse into a trot.

As the men reached the campsite, Bluebird emerged from the bushes. She ran to Levi to grab his revolver, but Lucky jumped from his horse and grabbed her before she could get hold of the gun. He flung her to the ground and drew his pistol.

"You stay right there, or I'll shoot you," Lucky yelled before reaching down and retrieving Levi's revolver. Levi opened his eyes as he became cognizant of the sound of a man's voice. He saw Lucky peering down at him. He started to speak, but then closed his eyes and remained silent.

Everett scrambled over to Levi and Bluebird's saddles and plucked the rifles from the scabbards. "This is an interesting situation," he said.

"What's wrong with him?" Lucky asked Bluebird.

"Rattlesnake bite," Bluebird answered.

"I wouldn't wish that on my worst enemy. Do as you're told, or we'll kill him. We'll be gone in the morning. Fix us some food," Lucky ordered.

Bluebird stirred the coals remaining in the campfire and added some sticks. Once she had a flame, she pulled some salt pork from Levi's saddlebag and plopped the meat into the skillet.

"After we eat, we just might have to have some fun with that Injun. I've always wanted have a go with one of them," Everett said.

"We'll do no such thing. I might have sunk to horse thieving, but I'll not be part of that," Lucky said.

"Ah, they're all like dogs in heat. They want it and don't care where they get it," Everett protested.

"Everett, just shut up," Lucky ordered.

Everett stalked off to the creek. Lucky kept an eye on Bluebird.

By the time the meat had cooked, Everett had returned and taken a seat by the fire. Bluebird handed the men plates, letting them retrieve the pork for themselves. As the men ate, she walked over to check on Levi.

"Where are you going?" Lucky asked.

"I help Levi," Bluebird said.

"Get back over here," Lucky ordered.

"I help Levi," she restated, ignoring the command.

Lucky studied the Indian for a moment before deciding to let things be.

Bluebird made a fresh poultice and applied the leaf paste to Levi's swelling leg. The punctures were an angry red and oozing. She demanded he drink some water, but he refused at first.

"I'm sorry, Bluebird. I've let you down," Levi whispered.

"You be fine. I'm okay," she said, trying to sound stronger than she felt. She had seen many men make a full recovery from a rattler bite—and she'd also seen a fair share of them die. The thought of Levi dying scared her. Not only would she be left on her own, but she also realized her heart would ache for the man she'd come to know. The two men in camp were also a problem. She understood enough English to know they had talked of raping her. She figured they'd kill her and Levi if they did.

"You'll," Levi corrected with a forced smile.

"You'll be fine," Bluebird said. She removed the shirt from his head and walked to the creek to soak it.

Lucky and Everett kept an eye on her as she bent over toward the water.

"That's a fine-looking Injun. I don't know why you don't want some of it," Everett said.

Lucky didn't answer. He watched as Bluebird returned and delicately rewrapped Levi's head. She walked to the campfire and sat down across from him. He had to admit that Everett was right about her looks. An aching for the pleasures of a woman stirred in him, and he contemplated Everett's words about squaws being like dogs in heat.

∞

Caleb and Joey knew they were getting close to finding Leif, because the tracks now showed little wisps of a fresh dust trail. The men had skipped breakfast and headed off at the first sign of light. They had pushed their horses hard in hopes of catching the thieves before they arrived in Cheyenne. Joey was hell-bent on serving up justice without getting the law involved.

The men abruptly pulled their horses to a stop at the spot where the hoofprints veered off the trail.

Caleb climbed off Diablo and examined the tracks. "I know darn well those tracks were made today and not last night before they made camp. What do you think they're up to?"

"I don't have a clue. Seems kind of early to be stopping to water the horses. Maybe they feared too many eyes upon them as they got close to town and decided to go in off the beaten path," Joey reasoned.

"Let's find out," Caleb said as he mounted his horse.

The trail of trampled grass was easy to follow. They trotted their horses to the tree line and followed the tracks along the creek. As they came around the bend, the sight of Lucky, Everett, an Indian, and a man lying on the ground so surprised Caleb and Joey that their horses bumped into each other as they yanked the reins. Lucky and Everett looked just as shocked by the turn of events when they caught sight of them. They ran for the cover of the rock ridge where Levi had been bitten. Bluebird stood frozen for a moment, confused by what was happening. She watched the three men turn their horses into the cover of the trees at the bend in the stream and disappear. Fearing for Levi, she managed to drag him behind a bush. From there, she could also see Lucky and Everett crouched behind the rocks.

"What do you think that Indian and man on the ground were all about?" Caleb asked after they tied the horses.

"I don't know. Be careful not to shoot them. They may not have a thing to do with this," Joey said.

"I'm not about to shoot a woman and a defenseless man. Do you know that man with Lucky?" Caleb asked with a touch of irritation.

"His name is Everett Clancy. He's about as useless as Lucky," Joey replied.

The men moved to the edge of the tree line, and each took cover behind a tree. They could see the Indian through the brush, lying next to the sick man. Lucky and Everett were completely concealed. Bullets began flying into the trees.

"How are we going to hit them if we can't see what we're shooting at?" Nils asked.

"I don't think they can see us either," Joey remarked.

Caleb moved away from his cover. "I'm going to wade the creek and see if I can get behind them. Otherwise, this will never end. We'll still be sitting here at dark wondering what they're doing. You two return fire to keep them occupied."

"Son, be careful," Nils pleaded.

"Don't worry, Daddy. I have a future bride waiting for me," Caleb said with a wink.

Joey and Nils began firing their rifles into the bushes as shots thudded around them. Caleb stepped into the water and crouched over as far as his longs legs would allow. Grimacing as the water soaked through his boots, he followed the stream around the abrupt bend. From there, he had a side view of Everett and Lucky in their positions behind the rocks. The outlaws were too preoccupied to notice his arrival.

Caleb aimed his revolver at Everett. "Throw down your guns," he yelled.

Everett stood and swung his revolver toward the voice. Caleb didn't hesitate. He drilled two shots into the horse thief's chest. The bullets drove Everett backward into Lucky's line of fire, and his accomplice put a third bullet into his back that had been intended for Caleb. Before Everett toppled over, his body provided cover for Lucky to slip behind a large rock in the middle of the creek. Caleb, needing to take cover, sprinted out of the creek and dove behind a tree just as Lucky's shots began to tear off chunks of bark.

Bluebird watched Everett die. Lucky now had his back to her. She had no idea whether the new attackers were friends or foes, but she knew the man behind the rock was an enemy. She got to her feet and dashed toward him. Lucky never heard her until it proved too late. Bluebird jumped onto his back. She sank her teeth into Lucky's ear and locked her arms around his neck in a stranglehold. Lucky let out a loud squeal and stood. He spun around wildly like a top, trying to throw the Indian off his back.

Caleb watched the whole episode unfold. He couldn't get a shot off for fear of hitting the Indian, so he sprinted to aid the woman. Before Caleb reached them, Lucky reached behind his back and ripped Bluebird from her death grip. He flung her into the rocks like a doll. As Lucky pointed his gun at Bluebird, Caleb began firing. He emptied his gun into the outlaw's back in an attempt to save the Indian. Lucky spun and eyed his former coworker a moment before dropping beside the Indian—he hadn't had the chance to fire his gun again.

Bluebird rolled onto her knees and then pressed her face into the ground, her hands clutching her head. She sounded as if she were cursing in her native tongue.

"Do you speak English?" Caleb asked as he knelt beside the Indian.

"Yes."

"How badly are you hurt?" he asked.

"Head hurts," Bluebird answered as she rubbed the back of her skull.

"Here, let me help you sit up," Caleb said as he gently placed his hands on her shoulders.

Bluebird didn't resist. She sat up. She had tears in her eyes that she quickly brushed away in embarrassment. Caleb reached over and felt the lump on the back of her head.

"That's a nasty bump. I'm Caleb," he said as he touched his chest, thinking she might be too naive to understand his meaning. "What's your name?"

"Bluebird," she answered. "Are you bad man, too?"

Caleb smiled. "No. These two men stole my horse. We came to get it back. We won't hurt you, I promise."

Bluebird nodded her head slowly to prevent any more pain. As she stood, she wobbled and had to grab Caleb by the arm to steady herself. "I need to help Levi."

Caleb cupped his free hand to his mouth and yelled, "We're okay here. We are walking out."

"Okay. We're coming," Joey hollered back.

"What happened to Levi?" Caleb asked.

"Rattlesnake bite," Bluebird answered. She tried taking a step but couldn't get her balance.

"I'm carrying you," Caleb said. He scooped her up into his arms before she could protest.

He gently carried Bluebird to the campsite and deposited her by the fire. Joey and Nils jogged up and helped Caleb carry Levi to his bedroll. Getting on her hands and knees, Bluebird inhaled deeply to clear her head before crawling to Levi. As she felt his forehead, Levi opened his eyes and braved a smile.

"We are safe," she said.

"Good," Levi said before exhaling and closing his eyes.

Grabbing the canteen, Bluebird said, "Drink some water."

"You're getting awfully bossy," Levi managed to say before the canteen was pressed to his lips.

As the men watched Bluebird shove leaves into her mouth, Caleb explained what had happened. Joey took particular delight in hearing how the Indian had chomped Lucky's ear. The men exchanged puzzled glances, though, when Bluebird spit the leaf paste into her hand and applied it to the snakebite.

Nils had never seen such a thing. He walked to Bluebird and squatted down next to her.

Joey and Caleb strolled over to Leif to check on the animal. The horse looked none the worse for wear. It nickered at them.

"So what's their story?" Joey asked, nodding his head toward Levi and Bluebird.

"I don't know yet. I guess we'll have plenty of time to find out. We've already missed our own weddings, and we can't leave them. She can't walk straight, and I'm not sure he's going to make it," Caleb replied.

"I'll let you do all the explaining to Claire and Caroline when we get back to the ranch," Joey said as he patted Caleb on the back.

Chapter 8

Some of the swelling had gone out of Levi's leg by the following morning. The area around the wound tingled with numbness, and his whole leg still throbbed, but nothing like the day before. Levi possessed little strength. He suffered through bouts of the chills where he would burrow into his bedroll. He did manage to sit up long enough to get some breakfast eaten, and he was able to keep the food down. Afterward, he went back to bed and slept.

Bluebird had regained her equilibrium, but still had a raging headache. The pain persisted as the day went on. She finally fetched the coffeepot and Levi's knife, then marched to the creek to get some fresh water and to find a willow tree. Several of the trees lined the creek; Bluebird chose one of the bigger ones. With the knife, she carved an eight square into its side deep enough to penetrate the outer and inner bark. She then used the blade to work the bark loose. With water and bark in hand, she headed back to camp and began heating the coffeepot. She whittled off chunks of the pink inner bark and dropped them into the heating water.

Nils watched Bluebird the whole time. He found the Indian woman and her use of plants and trees fascinating.

"May I ask what you are making?" Nils asked.

Bluebird hesitated a moment as she thought of the white man's words she needed to use. "Willow-bark tea. Make head quit hurting."

"I need to learn how to do this," Nils mused.

She let the water boil for about twenty minutes before removing the coffeepot from the fire. Levi had an extra kerchief in his saddlebag, and Bluebird retrieved it. She used the bandana to strain the tea into a tin cup. Nils eagerly watched the proceedings and was surprised to see the liquid come out nearly blood red. After the tea had cooled, she drank a whole cup of the brew.

Bluebird decided the tea might be good for Levi and brought a cup to him. "Drink this," she ordered.

"What is it?" Levi asked.

"Tea."

"Why? I'm about tired of chewing on leaves and whatnot," he said.

"Because I'm your ... momma, and I said so," Bluebird said, grinning with pride at her joke.

Levi let out a loud laugh in spite of how he felt. He'd never imagined Bluebird to be capable of humor. In fact, he'd never considered any Indian to have a sense of humor. They seemed always to be either angry or stoic. He took the cup and sipped the tea.

"Thank you for taking care of me. Your medicine probably saved my life," he said.

"Had to. Nowhere to go if you die," she said, her eyes twinkling with mischief.

"Oh. I thought maybe you liked me."

"You fine for a white man," she teased.

Levi smiled up at Bluebird. The more he got to know her, the more she proved full of surprises. He realized now how silly he had to been to think that Indians might not possess emotions. And learning that she had a sense of humor was nothing short of another revelation.

He reached up and took her hand. "Seriously, Bluebird, thank you."

"You are welcome, Levi. You rest now," Bluebird said before returning to the campfire.

"May I taste it?" Nils asked.

Bluebird had already decided she liked Nils. He had a kind face, and he was the first white man she had ever seen who took an interest in the Indian ways. She'd also come to understand he was the father of the one who killed the bad men. Nils had to be a strong man to have raised a son with such courage. She poured the remainder of the tea and handed the cup to him.

Nils took a small sip. "That doesn't taste half bad. A little sugar, and it'd be almost pleasant. Thank you, Bluebird."

Bluebird nodded her head and then decided she should practice her English. She decided to try a phrase she'd heard a white woman use one time. "My pleasure, Nils," she said.

Joey rode into camp an hour later, having returned from his trip to Cheyenne. He had gone to pick up some supplies and send a telegram to Claire to let her know they would be returning in a few days with Leif. Joey had taken Nils's horse on his trip. The animal was loaded with packages tied to the saddle.

"I figured we might as well eat good while we're here. I even bought two dozen eggs. I figured that they might sit well with Levi," Joey said as he climbed off his horse.

"Well, start fixing them. I'm hungry," Caleb said.

"You know that I'm the foreman of the ranch and that you still work for me. Don't be getting any ideas that you can run over me just because I'm becoming your stepdaddy-in-law," Joey said.

Caleb let out a laugh. "I've gotten used to the idea of you marrying Claire, but this is the first time it's dawned on me that you'll be Caroline's stepdad. That should make for some interesting father-daughter talks."

"I have no reason to believe that it will make her any less hardheaded or easier to reason with," Joey said before retrieving the basket of eggs and a package of bacon. "I guess we'll have breakfast for supper."

As Joey and Bluebird began cooking the meal, Caleb noticed that Levi was sitting up on his bedroll. Caleb strolled over and sat down beside him.

"How are you feeling?" Caleb asked.

"Like I just might live. That Indian medicine must work," Levi answered. He held out his hand to shake with Caleb. "I want to thank you for what you did yesterday."

"Good. Glad to hear you're feeling better. I was just trying to get my horse back," Caleb said modestly.

"Well, you sure helped us out."

"Is Bluebird your wife?"

"No . . ." Levi said, drawing out the vowel. "I helped her out of a bad situation. She didn't have anywhere to go, and I couldn't just leave her."

"Where are you headed?"

"I don't know. I thought I could find a job in Cheyenne, but nobody would hire me. I have no idea what we're going to do. No ranch will hire me with her tagging along, and I don't think I could look at myself in the mirror if I abandoned her," Levi said.

"What are you good at?" Caleb asked.

"I did some blacksmithing in my youth. I've spent most my life in a saddle, and I'm a pretty fair shot. I've never, ever wanted to settle down before now. So to be honest, I guess I'm not good at much of anything," Levi replied.

"That bacon smells good. Let's badger Joey to hurry up with cooking," Caleb said before helping Levi to his feet.

The willow-bark tea had taken the edge off the pain in Levi's leg. He still didn't have much appetite, so he spent more time asking questions about the Langley ranch than he did eating.

Bluebird felt better also. She'd never been around a group of civil white men before. She listened intently to their conversations, trying to comprehend as much of it as possible.

After they finished eating the meal and the skillet and plates had been scrubbed, Caleb said, "Joey, I need to stretch my legs and walk off some of this dinner. Let's take a stroll."

Joey loaded his pipe with tobacco and struck a match, then the two men walked toward the road. Neither spoke until they were well away from the others.

"So what's on your mind?" Joey asked.

Caleb first explained Levi and Bluebird's situation. "Bluebird seems like fine person, and I believe Levi is ready to grow some roots. I was wondering what you thought about hiring Levi to take Lucky's spot and letting them live in the old cabin," he said.

Surprised, Joey raised his eyebrows as he looked at Caleb. "We don't really need to replace Lucky. The only reason we hired him was that we needed more bodies during our war with Nathan Horn," he said.

"I know, but after things settle down, I want for me, you, Claire, and Caroline to sit down and talk about the ranch's future. I think we need to diversify and get into cattle. You and I already saw with our own eyes the closing of Fort Kearny in Nebraska, and once the army whips the Indians around these here parts, they're liable to shut down Fort Laramie, too. We'll have a lot of horses and nobody to sell them to. More settlers will be coming and needing beef," Caleb said.

"Those are all valid points, but I don't think Caroline would ever agree to that. She'll want to keep the ranch just like her daddy envisioned it," Joey said.

"You're probably right. And it's Claire and Caroline's decision to make, but I just want them to think about it," Caleb said.

Joey took a puff from his pipe and blew out the smoke. "If we were to hire Levi, I don't know what we'd do with all things stored in the cabin."

"I looked in there the other day. Half of that stuff could be pitched. We could move the rest of it to the shed where we keep the buggy and cover it with tarps," Caleb said.

"You've really thought this out. Levi must have really made an impression upon you."

"I suppose so. I can tell he's a lot sharper than Lucky—or Reese, for that matter. But mainly I got to thinking about what a fix I'd have been in if you hadn't taken me under your wing. I'd just like to pass that generosity on down," Caleb replied.

"Have you ever discussed Indians with Caroline?" Joey asked.

"I know they killed her daddy, but that's about it, I guess."

"Caroline is scared to death of Indians—all Indians."

"Really? Well, maybe it's time she gets over it. I know Indians are raised way different than us, but they're still just people under their red skin," Caleb reasoned.

Joey took another puff off his pipe and exhaled loudly. "I fear Caroline will be rankled like an old wet hen, but if you really want this, I'll go along with you. But just so you know, I have a feeling there's a whole lot more to the story of Levi and Bluebird than you've been told."

"Could be. Thanks, Joey. We better turn back before it gets dark," Caleb said.

Caleb waited until the next morning to offer Levi a job. The young man was so excited, he would have danced a jig if not for the bad leg.

Bluebird also looked relieved to hear the news. After learning of the Langley ranch, she had hoped they might offer Levi work. Her general perception of white men had changed dramatically since being rescued. She had considered Levi the exception to most palefaces, but had now come to accept that there might be more honorable ones than she had once imagined.

Levi insisted he could ride the following day. Truth be told, he felt weak and his leg still throbbed, but he figured he could at least stay in the saddle. He was starting to get jumpy, worried that the Shumans would show up. He didn't want to chance endangering himself, Bluebird, or his new friends by lingering any longer. Fort Laramie was far enough away that he doubted the outlaws would ever find them there. Though he no longer felt any animosity toward Bluebird for being an Indian, and had come to like her, he had no idea what to make of the notion that they would be sharing a cabin together. He wondered if he would have to spend the rest of his life with her as retribution for his past sins.

Bluebird could see that Levi still didn't feel well. He had dark circles under his eyes and his cheeks were drawn. She had serious doubts he would be capable of riding all day. While the others were making coffee and fixing breakfast, she slipped over to his bedroll and sat down beside him.

"You not ready to ride," Bluebird said.

"We need to get out of here. The Shumans could find us. I'll be fine," Levi said in a lowered voice.

"We should tell Caleb and Joey," she said.

"No. They might just leave us if they learn the bad things I've done, and I'm in no shape to defend us. This is a chance to start over for both of us. We have to get out of here," he said.

Bluebird looked Levi in the eyes and realized they no longer looked as they once had. The hardness they had held had all disappeared. Levi's heart had changed. "I take care of you."

"Breakfast is ready," Joey announced.

After the meal, Caleb kicked out the campfire. While the others were packing up, he walked over to the two graves they had dug. Lucky and Everett and their burial sites would all be lost to history by the time the grass grew back over the freshly turned soil. Caleb felt bad for Lucky, even if he had stolen Leif. The ranch hand had not been particularly smart or good at his job, but Caleb had never wished him any ill will. He certainly never imagined he might end up killing him. He paused a moment longer before turning away and retrieving his saddle off the ground.

Joey, sensing Caleb's mood, came over and put his arm around his friend. "We got to get home and get ourselves fitted for wedding coats," he said with a grin.

Chapter 9

September 21, 1877

The return trip to the Langley ranch proved uneventful, except that Levi slowed the group's travel. He never complained, but one of the others, usually Caleb or Bluebird, would notice him struggling and call for a rest. Levi felt better and most of the swelling had gone out of his leg, but he had no stamina. The trip took an extra day than they planned, but nobody complained. Nils used the time to learn everything he could about Bluebird's culture. Bluebird was enthralled with Nils's fatherly ways. She readily talked with him, using the time to practice her English.

Caroline, Claire, and Olivia were sitting on the porch sipping tea when the group arrived home. Joey thought the expressions on the women's faces when they noticed a new man and an Indian among them were priceless. Claire looked mildly amused while Caroline looked shocked and apprehensive. He dreaded the conversation that would be coming later.

"Ladies, it's good to be home," Joey said. "I'd like you to meet Levi Bolander and Bluebird. I hired Levi to take Lucky's place. We're going to put them up in the bunkhouse for tonight. Tomorrow, we'll clean out the cabin so they can stay there."

Caroline's eyes grew large, and she set her jaw. Even Claire looked as if she were a bit taken aback by the news.

Caleb looked over at Joey in disbelief. He hadn't expected his friend to take the fall for hiring Levi.

"I see. We can discuss all that at supper," Caroline said before realizing that Joey had forgotten to introduce them. "I'm Caroline. This is my mother, Claire, and this is Caleb's mother, Olivia."

"Pleased to meet you all," Levi said, tipping his hat.

Bluebird had listened to enough conversations around the campfire to know that Joey and Caleb would soon be marrying the mother and daughter. She had also picked up on the fact that Caroline could be difficult to deal with. Bluebird looked into Caroline's eyes. She not only saw anger, but fear. Caroline looked as if she were scared of her. Nobody had bothered to mention that. The situation made Bluebird feel as she had whenever Ellis had taken her to town—all the white women would point at her and drag their children across the street away from her.

Caleb climbed off his horse. "Give me a hug," he said to Caroline.

Caroline embraced him. "I'm glad you're home and safe," she said.

Joey was anxious to get out of the saddle and get the argument out of the way. "We'll get the horses put up and everybody settled before we come inside the house. Boy, do we have some stories to tell you."

After the horses were fed, Levi and Bluebird were introduced to Dan and Reese and left in their care.

As the men were walking to the house, Joey said, "You let me deal with Caroline. There's no need for her to be mad at you, too."

"I never planned on you taking the blame for Levi," Caleb said.

"I know, but I am the foreman. It is my job to decide how many ranch hands we need. Caroline will accuse you of trying to take over things if she knows it was your idea. I've really been her daddy figure ever since Jackson died, so she'll get over this faster if it's just coming from me," Joey said.

The women were busy preparing supper when the men entered the kitchen and took seats at the table.

Caroline grabbed a towel and wiped the flour from her hands. She spun around to face the table. Her shoulders were pulled back defiantly, and her head was tilted back slightly. "When did we decide we needed to replace Lucky?"

"I guess when I decided that Levi would be a good ranch hand," Joey replied.

"We have always decided those things together."

"Well, you weren't with us to discuss it."

Caroline looked around the room. She wasn't really comfortable arguing in front of Nils and Olivia, but her anger wouldn't wait for a more opportune time. "And since when did we start hiring ranch hands who come with women and giving them their own cabins? I wonder what Dan and Reese think about that."

"As long as they are getting paid, I don't see where it's really any of Dan and Reese's concern," Joey replied.

Caleb took off his hat and ran his fingers through his hair. "Levi and Bluebird are not a couple, Caroline. He helped her out. Neither had anywhere to go."

"Just as I suspected—you had a hand in this nonsense, too. You don't know a thing about those two. They could have made up any story," Caroline accused.

Claire stepped beside her daughter. "You need to calm yourself. Right or wrong, this is not the end of the world."

"Not the end of the world? This Bluebird is an Indian. For all we know, her tribe could swoop in and kill every last one of us. Did you forget that Indians killed Daddy?" Caroline asked.

Nils had watched the argument unfold with the notion that the whole thing was no more than a family spat, but the disparaging of Bluebird riled him. "I don't want in the middle of this, but I feel compelled to defend Bluebird. I've spent a lot of time with her in the last few days, and I can assure you that she is a noble woman. She is from the New Mexico Territory. She doesn't even know where her people are now. She confided in me about her life, and I can assure you that if you knew her circumstances, you would feel nothing but compassion for her—at least I would hope so."

The rebuke by Nils caught Caroline so off guard that she didn't know what to say. Her face colored with embarrassment, and an uncomfortable silence hung in the room. She now realized where Caleb got his ability to back a person into a corner and leave them defenseless.

"You are right. I do not know Bluebird and I shouldn't make assumptions about her. But I can't help the fact that I'm scared of Indians. I also know Joey hired Levi because he felt sorry for him, and we don't need another ranch hand."

Claire gently grasped her daughter's elbow. "We survived with Lucky on the payroll and we'll survive with Levi, too. And I for one am glad to have somebody in the old cabin. We'll have to keep it fixed up that way. It reminds me of the old days. Some pretty special memories got created inside those walls. I think you and I should count our blessings that we're marrying two men who choose compassion over money. Now, let's get supper fixed. I'm dying to hear all about the trip," she said as she coaxed Caroline back toward the flour.

With the argument successfully ended, the women returned to cooking. Just before serving the food, Claire brought out a couple of bottles of wine to celebrate the men's return and to soften any bruised egos.

Caroline knew she'd been bested. She decided not sulk at the table, though she resented being ganged up on. She had had a hard enough time getting her way before Joey and her mother had gotten romantically involved—and before Caleb had showed up at the ranch. It seemed that, from then on, everything would be a four-way decision. She had no doubt that she would be the one usually coming up short. As she watched Caleb animatedly telling of how Bluebird chomped down on Lucky's ear, she couldn't help but smile. A surge of love coursed through her, and she reminded herself that happiness and compromise beat loneliness and control any old day.

Once Joey and Caleb had finished telling their tales of the trip, the normally reticent Nils launched into an account of the things he'd learned from Bluebird. He talked in detail about her treatment of the rattlesnake bite and her potion for treating headaches. Olivia listened with amusement at her husband's obvious fascination with the Indian culture. Thirty-five years of marriage made her feel secure in her role as Nils's wife, otherwise, she thought she just might be jealous of the Indian woman.

After the meal, Caleb and Caroline excused themselves and stepped outside. The sun sat halfway below the horizon, and the air had already started to cool. Caleb put his arm around Caroline's shoulders and pulled her close as they walked.

"So do you still love me?" Caleb asked.

"I do. I figured you pulled this hiring-of-Levi trick to try to make one last attempt at getting out of marrying me," Caroline teased.

"Never," Caleb replied and swept Caroline into his arms. His kissed her passionately. "I missed you."

"I missed you, too. We'd be married by now if not for all of this. We need to hurry up so I can make Mother a widow again," Caroline jested.

"Don't blame Joey. I was the one that talked him into hiring Levi," Caleb pleaded.

"I know you were. I was just kidding, but I do feel kind of ganged up on sometimes. My daddy and mother built this ranch from the ground up, but I have less and less say about matters as time goes on around here."

"You know Joey and I have no intentions of taking over things. Honestly, Levi and Bluebird seem like good people who just need a chance. Kind of like when I first showed up out here."

"I suppose. But Caleb, I can't help it that I'm scared of Indians. I have no control over how I feel toward them. My heart starts racing and my chest gets tight every time I see one of them."

Caleb tilted his hat off his forehead. "Well, Daddy is sure enamored with Bluebird, and I consider him to be a pretty fair judge of character. Maybe you'll find out the same if you give her a chance," he said.

"I don't know if I can do that. Does she act like a savage?"

"No, not at all. She struggles with English some, and I'm not saying she acts just like we do, but after a while, you quit thinking about her being an Indian. She's hard not to like," Caleb replied.

"I have a hard time imagining that I'll ever be able to do that. We better get back inside before you get the urge to drag me into the woods. You have that gleam in your eye," Caroline joked before taking Caleb's hand and leading him back toward the house.

"It's not what I have in my eye that you need to worry about," Caleb said, causing them to burst into laughter.

Chapter 10

Langley Ranch

September 22, 1877

Having previously made arrangements with Captain Tyrone Willis to give Nils and Olivia a tour of Fort Laramie, Claire convinced Caleb to take his father and mother there for the day so that he could spend some alone time with them. Claire recruited everyone else on the ranch to help with cleaning out the cabin. Readying the old log home for inhabitants turned into a bigger ordeal that anyone had imagined. Claire rummaged through boxes and drawers, holding up the proceedings every time she stopped to reminisce. The men, except for Levi, carried out the contents and either stored them in the shed or threw them in the burn pile. Levi and the women busied themselves washing the walls and cabinets.

Claire treated Levi and Bluebird as if she had known them all their lives. She tried to draw them out in conversation. Levi talked readily, but managed to give away little about his past life.

Bluebird felt an instant bond with Claire. The ranch matriarch's sense of humor and commanding presence reminded the Indian woman of her own mother. She doubted she'd ever be close to the daughter, but hoped to spend time with Claire.

Caroline attempted to be friendly and welcoming, but her discomfort around Bluebird made it hard for her to relax. She busied herself with scrubbing a wall away from the others.

The men were carrying lumber to the shed when Claire and Levi headed to the bunkhouse for some supplies. Bluebird decided to use the moment to approach Caroline. She was a couple of steps away when the ranch owner noticed her. Caroline startled and covered her mouth to stymie a cry.

Bluebird stopped and did not move any closer. "I not mean to scare you. I'm sorry Indians killed your father. I wish you no harm."

Caroline removed her hand from her mouth and patted her hair. She subconsciously leaned back to put distance between herself and the Indian woman. After looking at Bluebird a moment, Caroline decided that honesty was the only course to take. "I know you don't. I was with Joey when we found Daddy. I saw what the Indians did to him, and I've never gotten over that. I don't mean to be this way. I really don't, but I can't help it. It left me scared of all Indians."

A sense of dread came over Bluebird, and her shoulders sagged a little. She wondered if she'd ever find a home. "You should not fear in your home. Maybe I go south to find Laguna people," she said.

For a moment, Caroline felt confused. Then it dawned on her that Bluebird was talking about her tribe. "No, that's too far to travel by yourself. Everyone likes you. I don't want to disappoint them by running you off the ranch. I'll try to do better, but I need some time. Please don't think badly of me. I don't like being this way."

Bluebird nodded her head before returning to the cabinets to scrub some more. She turned back toward Caroline and said, "You marrying a good man. He very brave."

"Thank you. Yes, he is," Caroline replied before deciding she must force herself into attempting conversation if she was ever going to face her fears. "Caleb says that Levi is a good man, too. Do you like him—in a man and woman kind of way?"

"Indians killed his family, too. He like you—he don't like Indians. He good to me because he has good heart," Bluebird replied.

Caroline was taken aback for a moment as she tried to think of something to say. "Caleb and I didn't like each other at all at first. Sometimes things change."

Levi and Claire returned to the cabin, ending any further discussion. Claire looked over at her daughter. Intuition told her something had gone on while she was out. She just hoped that Caroline had not done anything to further complicate the delicate situation.

By the end of the day, the cabin had been transformed back to its original purpose. Two cots were carried over from the bunkhouse. Extra cooking utensils and food were gathered from the house. Everyone stood around, eyeing their accomplishments and bragging about the cabin's appearance.

"What be my job?" Bluebird asked.

The question caused a pause in the conversations. Claire looked over at Joey to see him give a small shrug of the shoulders. Joey tried to think of something to say, but was at a loss for words. The notion of Bluebird helping on the ranch had never occurred to him.

"Can you cook?" Claire asked.

Bluebird nodded her head.

"She's a good cook," Levi added.

"Why don't you start fixing supper for the ranch hands each evening? That way they won't have to cook after they come in from working all day. You can also help me around the house with my rose bushes, the chickens, and such," Claire said.

"Thank you," Bluebird said.

"Everybody is tired. Let's let Levi and Bluebird get settled and call it a day. Thank you all for getting this done," Claire said.

After everyone filed out of the cabin, Levi dropped onto a cot. He'd put on a brave front throughout the day, but he felt exhausted. His leg throbbed from standing on it continuously.

"Are you fine?" Bluebird asked.

"Just tired. Do you think I will ever heal?" Levi wondered.

"Yes. Maybe next week, maybe next month. Rattlesnake bites like that."

"I have to carry my weight around here. They've given us a chance, and I can't let us down," Levi said.

"Caroline scared of me."

"Really? Why is that?"

Giving Levi a look as if the answer was the most obvious thing in the world, Bluebird said, "I stay away from her. She not bad—just scared."

"That's probably a good idea. One less thing to worry over and maybe she'll come around. I bet she didn't appreciate Caleb hiring me then," Levi said.

Bluebird squatted down beside the cot and brushed Levi's hair off his forehead. He pulled his head back from her. His eyes betrayed misgivings. She had grown very fond of him and wished he viewed her as more than just an Indian he felt obligated to help or one who had saved his life. The white race was a strange bunch, to her way of thinking. While Indians as a rule hated the whites, they were also occasionally capable of accepting them into the tribe as equals. She had her doubts that any white ever saw an Indian as their equal, though.

"I fix food. Make you strong," Bluebird said.

∞

Caleb returned with his parents from Fort Laramie. After Caroline inadvertently interrupted Bluebird's cooking to give Caleb a quick a peek at the cabin, the couple decided to go for a ride before supper. Spending the day in the midst of all the others had left her ready to escape for a little while. They followed the stream that ran through the ranch. Neither talked as they rode at a brisk trot. After a day of nonstop chatter, the quiet felt welcoming. They reached the grassy knoll where they had first made love, and stopped.

"Now that I've seen that cabin cleaned up, I'm starting to think we should have taken it," Caleb joked as he plopped down on the grass.

"It doesn't come with a cook, and Mother is much better at cooking than I am," Caroline said, taking a seat beside him.

"You're just afraid you might become domesticated."

"I domesticated you. That's accomplishment enough."

"Did being around Bluebird today ease your fears any?" Caleb asked.

"She came up to me when we were alone and told me she wished me no harm. I about jumped out of my skin. I'm sure she thinks I'm some kind of a crazy white woman. I guess it was a start, but I'm not sure. Mother somehow figured out that something happened and asked me all about it. I know it's wrong to judge Bluebird based on what happened to Daddy, but I really can't help it. Indians just plain scare me. I had nightmares about them coming for me in my bed for a year after Daddy died," Caroline replied.

"Just give it some time. I think she'll win you over."

"We'll see. I'm not sure you can win over irrational fear. Mother is announcing at church tomorrow that the weddings are rescheduled for next Saturday. You still have time to back out of marrying me."

"Shoot, I'm not backing out now. I'm just getting you trained proper. No need for me to start over from scratch with someone new. She probably wouldn't own a ranch either," Caleb said, grinning mischievously.

"Caleb Gunnar, you are getting awfully cocky," Caroline said before leaning over and kissing him.

"You know, we have time for a little romancing before we head back," Caleb suggested.

"Nope. You are officially out of luck until our wedding. It'll make the night more special. And besides, I'd die if we got back home and your mother saw some grass stuck on the back of my head," Caroline said.

Caleb chuckled. "I didn't know you could get your virginity back in a week."

Chapter 11

Langley Ranch

September 24, 1877

After lunch, Caleb and Joey rode their horses into Fort Laramie to be fitted for the wedding. Caroline and Claire had already selected the clothing for the men. They had chosen black cutaway sack coats with notched high lapels. The coats were worn buttoned only at the top to show off the vest underneath, and the women had selected black-and-white pinstriped ones. A high-collar white shirt, black tie, and black trousers completed the ensemble.

"I can't believe we're letting those women put us through this. Maybe they should be marrying bankers," Caleb said as he slipped into the coat.

"Quit your complaining. We're both lucky to have such fine gals willing to put up with us. I've never got to dress up like this before now," Joey said as the tailor began pinning the sleeve to the proper length on his coat.

"You sure look a lot different than the first time I ever laid eyes on you," Caleb said.

The two men began laughing so hard that their shaking bodies drew the ire of the tailor as he stabbed himself with a pin. When Caleb had happened upon Joey for the first time, the ranch foreman had been robbed by highwaymen and was walking down the road in only his faded-red long underwear and a derby hat.

"Hard to believe that was less than a year ago. So much has happened since then," Joey said when he regained his composure.

"It sure has. Who'd have thought the two of us would be getting hitched? That was about the last thing on my mind," Caleb said.

Once the tailor finished taking measurements, he gladly guided the two cowboys out the door and on their way.

"How about I buy you a beer? After this week, Caroline may never let you out of her sights again," Joey said.

"Sure. We deserve a drink after having to dress up like that," Caleb responded.

The two men walked into the Fort Laramie Saloon. As far as saloons went, this one looked pretty clean, and was lit better than most—but it still reeked of smoke and beer. A few soldiers were loitering around, along with some cowboys and regulars. Joey greeted those he knew as he and Caleb saddled up to the bar.

"Give us two beers, Ned," Joey said.

"Sure thing," Ned said before filling two mugs. "Have you wed Mrs. Langley yet?"

"This Saturday."

"You old dog. I never would have guessed in a million years that you'd ever get married," Ned said as he plopped the glasses onto the bar.

"Me either, Ned. Me either."

Ned leaned in close to the two men and said in a lowered voice, "That fellow sitting at the table in the corner with Howie Nickels claims to be Frankie Myers's brother. Says he's a bounty hunter from Arkansas and plans to find his brother's killer. I thought you two should know."

Frankie Myers had worked as a ranch hand for Nathan Horn. Caleb had had a run-in with the cowboy in the saloon and later killed him after the attempt on Caroline's life.

"That's interesting," Joey said before taking his first sip of beer.

Ned nodded his head at Caleb. "He heard about you breaking Frankie's hand, too."

"Thanks for the heads-up," Caleb said. He nonchalantly reached down and flipped the thong off the hammer of his Colt before taking a drink of beer.

Howie must have pointed Caleb out to the stranger. From the corner of his eye, Caleb could see the man get up from his chair and walk toward them.

"I'm Paul Myers, and Frankie was my brother. I hear that you're the fellow that stomped on his hand and made it about useless."

Caleb turned to face Paul. He could see the resemblance to Frankie as he looked down at the shorter man. They both possessed the same smart-alecky smirk. He looked as if he had just crawled out of some dark, rat-infested alley. "Frankie didn't mind his manners around a lady. I had to teach him a lesson," Caleb said.

"I didn't know ladies came into saloons."

"I have no quarrels with you. Just let it go," Caleb warned.

"Did you kill my brother?" Paul asked.

"From what I hear, the army never solved those mysterious deaths."

"Word I hear is that Frankie's boss had a feud with the ranch you work for," Paul said.

Caleb didn't say anything. He stared Paul in the eyes.

"Where are you from?" Paul demanded.

"I don't see where that's any of your concern," Caleb replied.

"I've lived down in Arkansas long enough to recognize the sound of a Southern boy when I hear one. Nobody around here knows a thing about you. Seems like you just blew in on the wind. From my years as a bounty hunter, I've come to learn that when a man just shows up somewhere out of the blue, he's likely got something to hide. I'll get to the bottom of this," Paul said before turning and walking back to his table.

Caleb took a sip of beer. "I think that went well, don't you?"

The two men finished their beers and headed for home.

Once they were out of town, Caleb said, "If he has a wanted poster on me and has half a brain, he's going to figure out who I am. I never figured I'd have to worry about somebody tracking me down all the way out here."

"I know."

"Maybe we should call off the wedding. I wouldn't want to bring shame to the Langley family. There's no need for Caroline to marry me just in time to see me hauled away. She's had enough bad luck with men," Caleb said.

"You're not doing that under any circumstance. We'll deal with that bounty hunter when the time comes if we have to," Joey said.

"Are you sure about this?"

"Caleb, you can't live your life worrying about what might come to be. A man that spends all his time worrying doesn't have time to actually live. And besides, most worries never come to anything in the first place. You've had enough setbacks in life," Joey said.

"But what if he tells the whole town of Fort Laramie that I'm a wanted man? I'll have everybody after me," Caleb said, clearly worried.

"I doubt bounty hunters are in the habit of sharing information on fugitives. It would be bad for business if somebody beat them to the bounty. Try to relax. Nothing has happened yet," Joey said, trying to sound more reassuring than he felt.

"Joey, even if this doesn't come to pass, I'm going to be looking over my shoulder the rest of my life," Caleb said.

"I don't know. I can't imagine many bounty hunters looking for fugitives from Tennessee coming all the way out here. This is just a bad coincidence," Joey said.

"We need to keep this to ourselves. There's no need to worry the women," Caleb said.

"Agreed."

"Do you think it was destiny that we met up on the trail, or just luck of the draw?" Caleb asked.

Joey raised his eyebrows in surprise as he glanced at his friend. "I'm not sure I'm smart enough to be talking philosophy with you, but I'm thinking it's all luck of the draw. What'd be the fun in living if our date of death was already penciled in the ledger? We've both seen men die in battle from the most unlucky of circumstances."

"I guess you're right. Life is hard to figure out sometimes," Caleb mused.

"On a happy note—are you going to name your first son after me since you would have never met Caroline without me?" Joey teased.

"Yeah, we're going to name him Faded Long John in honor of how you were dressed the first time I ever laid eyes upon you," Caleb said, giggling at his own joke.

"Shoo. You're never going to let me live down that day. You've gotten a lot of miles out of my misfortune. I do believe that the world has a way of evening things out and your day is coming," Joey said with a nod of his head.

Chapter 12

Langley Ranch

September 26, 1877

As long as Levi could work from the saddle, he felt well enough to help on the ranch. If he had to do much walking, he tired quickly. His ability to get along well with the others had eased his mind somewhat about the job. Dan and Reese had surprised him with their acceptance of a new ranch hand. He'd expected some resentment about the fact that he and Bluebird had been given the cabin to themselves, but had found none.

The one problem he was dealing with was not knowing squat about training the animals or roping them—being a good horseback rider alone wasn't enough.

"Have you ever roped at all before?" Joey asked when Levi tangled himself in his lasso and nearly tripped his horse.

"No, sir. I can't say that I have," Levi responded.

"Don't try it anymore until I teach you on foot in the corral. You're liable to kill yourself or your horse," Joey said.

Levi dropped his head and rubbed his chin. He despised failing. "I'm sorry."

"Nothing to be sorry about. Don't be getting all down in the mouth on me. We knew you lacked ranch hand experience when we hired you. Just remember what we teach you and you'll be fine," Joey said.

"Sure, I can do that."

"Dan and Reese, you two work on neck reining. I'm going to take Levi to the corral and work with him on roping," Joey said.

Joey and Levi rode to the corral. The ranch foreman patiently showed his pupil how to twirl the lasso above his head and point his hand at the target as he released the rope. Years of practice had made Joey an expert with a rope. He lassoed the post in the center of the corral every time.

Levi attempted to whirl the rope stiff-armed with little success. Joey had to show him how to flick his wrist. On his next attempt, Levi managed to get the rope twirling around his head, but when he released it, the lasso sailed well to the right of the post.

"Not bad," Joey said. "The next time, point all your fingers at the post as you release the rope. You let go of it too soon."

"Do you think I should just quit and get out of your hair? I don't want charity, or to be a burden on the ranch," Levi said.

"No," Joey said emphatically. "If you quit now, you'll make Caleb and me look bad, and we'll never hear the end of it from Caroline. You got some grit in you. Don't get discouraged so easily. We all had to start sometime."

"Caroline doesn't like me, does she?" Levi asked.

"She'll like you just fine when she sees you bring value to the ranch. Caroline has to be won over, but she's a great gal once you earn her trust. She hated

Caleb at first, and she's marrying him on Saturday, so there's plenty of hope for you. Now quit talking and start lassoing."

On Levi's fifth attempt, he lassoed the post. He grinned like a kid rewarded with a piece of candy for spelling all his words correctly on a test. "Maybe there is hope."

"That was near perfect. I'm going to go help the boys. You just keep practicing. Once it becomes second nature, we'll put you on a horse to try it. That's when you'll earn your spurs," Joey said before departing.

Levi spent the rest of the afternoon practicing. By the time the others returned from the pasture, his right arm felt as if it might fall off. His leg throbbed, but he'd improved his lassoing enough that he collared the fence post more times than not.

Bluebird had a stew ready to serve when the men entered the bunkhouse. She'd only been preparing their meals for two days, but Dan and Reese were already big fans of her cooking. They were appreciative of not having to do the chore themselves, especially since Joey now took his meals with Claire and wasn't fixing grub for them.

As they ate, Levi noticed that Reese appeared smitten with Bluebird. The ranch hand smiled at her constantly and tried his best to draw her out in conversation. Bluebird seemed to bask in the attention and did her best to answer the cowboy's questions. Levi liked Reese, but didn't appreciate the interest he paid to Bluebird. He wanted to remind the ranch hand that he was looking out for her and didn't need any help in the matter.

It never occurred to him that he might be actually jealous about the situation.

After the dishes were washed, Levi rebuffed Dan and Reese's attempts to get them to stay and play cards. He wanted to get Bluebird away from Reese. Making an excuse to get back to the cabin, he and Bluebird walked out of the bunkhouse.

"You better watch Reese. He's got eyes for you," Levi warned once they were in the cabin.

Bluebird smiled. "I like Reese. He is nice."

Levi made a sour expression. That was not the response he wanted. "He probably just wants to get you in the sack so he can say he tried an Indian."

Not understanding what he meant, Bluebird looked at Levi quizzically.

"He probably wants to take you to bed," Levi said.

"You . . . are mean. Why do you care?" Bluebird asked.

"I'm not trying to be mean. I just don't want you to end up with another man like Ellis. I'm trying to look out for you," Levi said.

"Reese not like Ellis."

"I don't know. We barely know him," Levi grumbled.

Bluebird sat down at the table and ran her hands down her long hair. "I think Harper and Jordan are coming."

"What? What makes you think that?" Levi asked.

"I don't know. I just feel them be close," Bluebird replied.

"You Indians go around acting like you're some mystical mind readers. I'm surprised you all don't join in with the snake oil peddlers and tell fortunes in every town," Levi complained.

Bluebird didn't understand a word of what Levi had just said, but she knew enough to know it was angry and hurtful. She set her jaw and stared at Levi with a stoic expression. Only her eyes gave her pain away by starting to well with tears.

In the light coming through the window from the setting sun, Levi could see Bluebird's eyes glisten. He let out a sigh and rubbed the back of his neck. He felt like a cad for what he had said. For the first time since deciding to change his life, he knew he'd failed in his vow.

"Bluebird, I'm sorry. I shouldn't have said those things. Seeing Reese flirt with you put me in a bad mood. Then the thought of the Shumans showing up and ruining everything made me uneasy. I took it out on you. I'm truly sorry," he said.

Bluebird started talking in her native tongue. Levi didn't have a clue what she was saying—and he had a hunch he didn't want to know. She talked rapidly, in an animated voice. He sat down at the table across from Bluebird and let her vent. Finally, she stopped talking.

"I don't know what you said, but I'm willing to listen if you try telling me," he said.

She sighed so loudly that Levi leaned back a little in his chair, expecting a tirade.

"You won't say why Reese make you mad. You . . . I don't know word. You like me but won't say so. You don't want Indian, but don't want me with Reese. I'm Indian, but my blood runs red like you," she said.

"'Jealous' is the word you wanted. You think I'm jealous that Reese likes you," Levi said. He paused and rubbed his chin as he processed Bluebird's words. "Maybe I am jealous. I don't know. You make me feel so confused. I think I should have stuck to robbing people and not caring about anything."

"You want to be good," Bluebird said.

"Yeah, you're right—I do. I'm sorry I hurt you. I'll do better. I promise," Levi said as he stood. "Do you want to go for a little walk?"

"Sure."

They walked down the ranch's driveway. The air was cooling quickly, and Bluebird walked with her arms folded against her breast.

"Tell me about your life before you were stolen," Levi said.

"Life happy until the white man started coming—wagon after wagon. Mexicans make trouble, but braves protected us until we lost many to the white man's guns. Mexicans come one night to steal young ones. I saw my father and mother die that night. They stole me and others," Bluebird said.

"I'm sorry," Levi said.

"You not to blame. You help me," she said, shivering from the cool air on her bare legs.

"I guess our lives weren't that much different. I wanted to be a lawyer when I was a boy," Levi said before picking up a rock and tossing it.

"What is lawyer?"

"Important man. Respected like a chief," he replied.

"You an important man to me," Bluebird said.

Levi smiled sadly. "Thank you, Bluebird. I'll certainly try to be one for you."

Chapter 13

September 29, 1877

The weather couldn't have been nicer for the wedding day. The sky appeared a cloudless robin's-egg blue and the sun had warmed away the morning chill. The house was in a state of pandemonium as six people readied themselves for the big day. Somehow, they all managed to leave for the church on time.

Caroline, Claire, and Olivia were huddled together in the room at the front of the church. Olivia busied herself with helping the other women put the finishing touches on their hair. Claire was in a festive mood, making jokes about being the oldest bride ever in Fort Laramie and giggling. Caroline felt nervous even if she didn't have any reservations about marrying Caleb. She loved him more than she had thought was possible, but the pain of her first marriage had left scars that would never go away. Taking a big breath, she tried focusing on the joy that Caleb brought to her life.

The two women wore matching ivory-colored cotton dresses with three-quarter-length sleeves, high ruffled necklines, V-shaped winged bibs, and bustles.

"You two look lovely. A stranger might think you two are sisters," Olivia said.

"Only if they needed spectacles," Claire joked.

Olivia faced Caroline and placed her hands upon the girl's shoulders. "Caroline, I couldn't be happier that Caleb and you are getting married. You have made that boy whole again. I never thought I would see that. I wish you all the happiness in the world—and some grandbabies down the road," she said and gave Caroline a wink.

Turning to Claire, Olivia said, "You and Joey have been wonderful hosts and have become dear friends. I will head back to Tennessee with much relief, knowing that Caleb has a wonderful new family here. You and Joey deserve the happiness you have found."

"You raised quite a son, Olivia. He's the best thing that's happened to this ranch in a long time. Thank goodness Caroline never succeeded in running him off. I don't know what we would have done without him. Everything that Caroline has brought to Caleb, he has likewise brought to her," Claire said.

"With Caleb unable to live back home, I couldn't have found a better place for him."

The sound of the piano drifted in from the church.

"I guess we better take our places," Caroline said.

Olivia took her seat with Nils while the two women walked outside and around to the front entrance. The women were serving as each other's maid of honor, and Caleb and Joey were each other's best man. Caroline cracked the door and peeked inside the church. The room was filled with church members, ranchers, and their wives. Dan and Reese had convinced Levi and Bluebird to accompany them, and the four sat in the second row of pews. Caroline snickered as she watched women nodding their heads toward Bluebird and gossiping. Caleb and Joey were standing in their places, looking more handsome than she had ever seen them. Caroline could feel her heart race. She actually felt swoony looking at Caleb. After taking such an instant dislike to him at their first meeting, she still had a hard time believing how much she had grown to love him. Taking one final glance, she decided that nobody could accuse the husbands-to-be of not cleaning up well.

The piano pounded out the first notes of "Wedding March," and it echoed through the room The crowd stood. Caroline walked down the aisle, followed by Claire.

Preacher Hobbs welcomed the attendees to the church and quickly moved on to the ceremony. He talked glowingly of each member of the wedding party. He'd only met Caleb twice, but still managed to heap praise on the young man's character and his relationship with Caroline. The preacher then talked of the sanctity of marriage before administering the vows. He wasted no time going through the proceedings.

"Gentlemen, you may kiss your brides," Preacher Hobbs said.

Joey, embarrassed by public displays of affection, attempted to get by with a peck, but Claire nixed that by kissing him like a woman laying claim to her man. Caleb and Caroline grinned at each other like two anxious teenagers before delving into an enthusiastic kiss.

"Ladies and gentlemen, I'd like to introduce you to Mr. and Mrs. Joey Clemson and Mr. and Mrs. Caleb Gunnar," the preacher announced.

Caleb and Joey turned red as they faced the crowd. Claire and Caroline both grinned as if they'd won the blue ribbon at the fair.

After the couples greeted all the well-wishers, they walked out into the churchyard to find that Dan and Reese had tied cans behind Claire's buggy and the rented carriage. The couples climbed into the buggies and, with a wave to the crowd, departed in different directions. Joey and Claire headed toward the ranch. Caleb and Caroline were staying at the Fort Laramie Hotel in town.

Nils and Olivia had come to the wedding on the buckboard wagon. They planned to spend the night at the hotel, but Claire would not hear of it. She insisted that the couples celebrate the evening in her home.

As they traveled toward Fort Laramie, Caleb held up his hand and looked at the ring on his finger. "I guess you're stuck with me now."

"You better believe it. I put too much training into you to let you ever get away," Caroline teased.

"Are you going to address Joey as your stepdaddy now?" Caleb asked, grinning.

Caroline made a face like she had bit into a green persimmon. "I didn't marry you for your sense of humor."

Between fits of giggles, Caleb said, "That may be best face I've ever seen you make. Everybody knows you think the world of Joey. I don't know why you act like you don't."

"Because he already struts around like he owns the place. I don't want him to start thinking I'm a pushover," Caroline said.

"I'm pretty sure that's about the last thought he'll ever entertain. He's mighty loyal to you," Caleb said.

"Oh I know. Don't be so literal. Joey and I keep each other on our toes. I doubt we'd have it any other way," Caroline said.

The couple reached Fort Laramie and left the carriage at the livery stable. As they were walking to the hotel, Caleb spied Paul Myers lounging in front of the saloon. Without saying anything, Caleb shepherded Caroline across the street and into the hotel before Myers saw him.

Caleb unlocked the door to their room and swept Caroline off her feet, causing her to let out a squeal. He carried her into the room and gave her a kiss before planting her on the bed.

"So, Mrs. Gunnar, what do you want to do now?" Caleb asked.

Attempting to speak with a Southern accent, Caroline said, "Why, Mr. Gunnar, as your wife, I believe it is my duty to submit to your wishes. Being a young woman who has been alone for a long time, I only hope you are capable of also satiating my wanton needs."

"Oh, I'm going to satiate you all right," Caleb said as he climbed into the bed amid an outbreak of giggles.

Chapter 14

Sunday morning found Caleb waking up later than usual in the hotel with Caroline's head resting on his shoulder and her leg hooked over his. He smiled at the thought that it had been years since he'd awakened in bed with a woman. The realization made him think of his late wife, Robin, for a moment. He would never totally get over losing her and the baby, but decided it best to banish such thoughts for this day. Turning his attention to Caroline, he ran his finger down her nose.

"Hey, sleepyhead. The morning's getting late," Caleb said.

Caroline opened her eyes and smiled up at Caleb. "Hello, husband. This bed feels awfully good. I think you wore me out too much to get out of it."

"I'm not sure I'm the one to blame, if my memory serves me well," Caleb said.

With a giggle and a kiss, Caroline said, "Well, if you insist . . . I think I can find the strength to please you one more time before breakfast."

After the couple made love, they headed downstairs and dined on bacon, eggs, and biscuits in the hotel dining room. Their meal got interrupted a couple of times by ranchers and their wives coming over to congratulate the newlyweds. When the waitress came to refill their coffee cups, she brought a large slice of chocolate cake and told them it was on the house to celebrate the couple's marriage.

Caleb paid for the meal, and then he and Caroline walked hand in hand to get the buggy. Feeling stuffed and tired, they strolled at a leisurely pace. Paul Myers was standing in front of the livery stable, talking to the blacksmith. Caleb tensed up at the sight of the bounty hunter and rubbed his chin. Caroline immediately sensed a change. Caleb unwittingly squeezed her hand. She looked up curiously at her husband.

"Stay out of the way if there's trouble. That's Frankie Myers's brother," Caleb said.

Myers turned from the blacksmith to face Caleb. "Well, I hear congratulations are in order. I'm impressed that a drifter can ride into town and marry a prominent rancher in short order."

Ignoring Paul, Caleb addressed the blacksmith. "Garland, we're ready for the buggy."

The blacksmith, sensing trouble, scurried into the stable.

"I'm talking to you. It ain't polite to ignore me," Paul said. "That pretty little wife of yours will think you're ill-mannered."

Caleb stared at Myers, but didn't speak.

"Suit yourself then," Paul said. "I didn't find you in my stack of posters, but I telegraphed the sheriff in Fort Smith to see if he has any that might be you."

"Are you finished?" Caleb asked.

Paul took two steps forward and used his index finger to tap on Caleb's chest. "Your day is coming. It's just a matter of time. I can smell a fugitive from a mile away, and I'm sure you killed my brother."

Caleb sent a jab straight into Paul's mouth, knocking the surprised bounty hunter back a step. Before Myers could recover, Caleb caught him with a left hook to the jaw so forceful that Paul's body twisted sideways. The rage that Caleb had never learned to harness had once again escaped its tether. His pulse quickened to the point where he could feel it thumping in his eardrums. He felt consumed with such fury that everything but inflicting pain was blocked from his mind. Some little weasel from Arkansas was trying to ruin his life after he'd found happiness again.

"Caleb, don't kill him," Caroline yelled to no effect.

Caleb grabbed his tormentor by the shirt and pants and hurled him into the street. As Paul tried to get to his feet, Caleb kicked him in the ass and sent him sprawling face-first into the dirt. Caleb bent down to retrieve Paul's revolver. He stood, putting his foot on top of Myers's head, and ground the sole of his boot into Paul's ear until the man hollered in pain.

"If you ever touch me again, I'll bury you beside that piece of trash brother of yours," Caleb threatened before walking away and throwing the revolver into the horse trough.

Taking Caroline by the arm, Caleb led her into the stable. They waited for Garland to finish hitching the wagon. Caroline patted Caleb on the arm in hopes of calming him. She'd seen him fly into a rage before and wasn't surprised by his actions. Her fear had been that he would kill the man and suffer the consequences.

Caleb helped her into the buggy. With a pop of the reins, they left the stable. Paul Myers was nowhere to be found when they pulled into the street.

"How long have you known he was in town?" Caroline inquired.

"Since Monday."

"And you and Joey decided that Mother and I didn't need to know this?" Caroline asked.

"That about sums it up. I thought about calling the wedding off, but Joey wouldn't hear of it. He said we'd deal with it if and when the time came. Myers is going to ruin everything," Caleb replied.

"Maybe he won't find out anything."

"Maybe, but he's got an ax to grind. He's knows I gave Frankie a beating and suspects I killed him."

"Joey was right. I wouldn't have let you off the hook that easily either. We will deal with it if the time comes," Caroline said.

"You can decide if you want to tell Claire, but I want to wait until Daddy and Momma leave tomorrow."

"Of course, but we do need to tell Mother. Her feelings were hurt enough when she found out we hadn't told her about your past."

They returned to the ranch to spend the rest of the day with Caleb's parents and Joey and Claire. Olivia and Claire were busy cooking steaks when the couple walked into the home. Nils had wanted a final tour of the ranch to see the mustangs one more time, and he and Joey had not yet returned.

The women greeted the newlyweds warmly, but Caleb could see in his momma's eyes that she was already dreading the parting that would come the following day. Even though he knew things had turned out better for him because he'd left Tennessee, he still felt guilt for abandoning his family. He gave his mother an extra-big hug.

"Olivia and I have decided that we want a baby here by the time the Bergs return this time next year. Olivia is ready for another one, and God knows I've waited long enough for a first one," Claire announced.

"Mother," Caroline chided.

"Don't 'mother' me. You know where they come from, and you're not getting any younger. We're putting you two on notice," Claire said.

Caleb glanced at the three women and decided to keep his mouth shut. He'd let Caroline handle this one.

"I'm not that old. Sometimes you're so embarrassing. You don't always have to speak your mind. Olivia isn't like you. I'm sure such talk makes her uncomfortable," Caroline said.

Olivia looked over at Claire. She admired the woman's daring and wished she possessed a little more of it. Emboldened by the other woman's actions, Olivia felt the urge to be audacious once in her life, just for the sake of it.

"Young lady, you heard your mother. We want a baby," Olivia said, smiling up at her son.

Chapter 15

October 1, 1877

Breakfast lacked its usual cheerfulness. Nils and Olivia would have to leave for town to catch the stagecoach as soon as they finished eating. Even Claire only halfheartedly tried to add some enthusiasm to the meal; she failed in her attempt anyway. Caleb and Caroline had planned to take his parents to town, but Olivia would not hear of it. She preferred to say her goodbyes in the intimacy of their friends' home rather than be seen getting teary-eyed on the street in front of strangers. Claire made an effort to give Nils money to pay for the carriage rental, but he wouldn't accept it. He insisted it was a small price to pay for all the hospitality the couple had been shown.

Caleb dragged the luggage out of the house and set it in the carriage as the couples gathered on the porch. Levi and Bluebird walked over from the cabin.

Bluebird removed a small leather pouch decorated in blue, yellow, and red beads from around her neck and placed it over Nils's head. "For you. We are friends."

"Yes, we are. It's been my honor to meet you," Nils said as leaned down and kissed her on the cheek. "I hope to see you next year."

Levi and Bluebird finished saying their goodbyes and headed toward the bunkhouse.

Joey shook Nils's hand and gave Olivia a hug. Claire and Olivia then embraced and started crying.

"You make sure you come back next year," Claire said.

"You've become such a dear friend in such a short time. I'll write you when we get home," Olivia promised.

Olivia threw her arms around Caroline. "You are everything I could hope for in a daughter-in-law. Take care of Caleb. And have a baby when you're ready. I was just kidding before—but I do want one before I get too old to enjoy it."

Caroline laughed as she returned the hug. "We'll work on that. I love you."

Nils hugged Caroline and said goodbye. She gave him a kiss and wiped her eyes as she moved beside her mother, leaving Caleb with his parents.

"I'm going to miss that view of those mountains. This is quite the land, and you've made a fine life for yourself here. I'm proud of you, son," Nils said as he embraced Caleb.

"Thank you, Daddy. I love you. Take care."

Caleb turned toward his mother. She stood before him, sobbing and looking pitiful. He hated seeing her cry. He felt helpless.

"Momma, I love you. Send Britt my love, too," Caleb said as he hugged her.

"I love you, too," Olivia said.

With a final goodbye, the couple boarded the carriage and departed. The others stood on the porch and watched until the buggy disappeared out of sight.

"Well, I guess this means it's back to work as usual," Joey said.

Caleb let out a sigh. "I'm afraid so," he said as he stared off into the distance.

Caroline patted her husband on the back. "I'll join you in a little while. I'm going to shuck this dress," she said before walking into the house with her mother.

In the bunkhouse, Joey issued assignments for the day. The men filed out to saddle their horses, leaving Bluebird by herself. Claire hadn't begun utilizing her around the house, and Bluebird felt bored with her only chore of cooking supper each night. Back in her teen years, before Mexicans kidnapped her, she had been quite good at making pottery. She contemplated seeing if she could still fashion pots and urns. She walked out of the bunkhouse with the intention of following the stream that ran through the ranch. She hoped to find a spot where the water cut into the bank and exposed a clay deposit.

Bluebird grabbed a wooden bucket from the cabin and set off along the stream. She had not yet explored the ranch, and walked at a leisurely pace as she took in the new sights and sounds. Her new home was different from her previous ones. It wasn't as rugged as the hideout in Colorado or as barren as her native land in New Mexico. Unable to find suitable clay, she continued over a mile downstream, into heavy pines. She started singing the old "Laguna Buffalo Dance" to pass the time. The faint smell of smoke stopped her in her tracks. As she looked around for signs of a fire, Jordan and Harper came charging out of the pines. She let out a squeal, dropped the bucket, and turned to run.

"I knew we'd find you," Harper yelled as he tackled Bluebird.

He landed on her with all his weight, knocking the wind from her. As she struggled to catch her breath, Harper grabbed her arms. Jordan did likewise with her feet. They carried Bluebird to their campsite and tied her with her back to a tree.

"We heard you singing. I thought you were a mute. You pulled a good one on poor old Ellis. Can you talk white man?" Jordan asked.

Bluebird shook her head.

"I bet I can make her learn it real quick," Harper said. He went to a tree and cut a switch. "Last chance to talk."

She again shook her head.

Harper began flogging Bluebird unmercifully. The stick made a swishing sound as it cut through the air and landed on her arms and legs, leaving angry-looking welts. Bluebird finally screamed, and Harper paused.

"You better talk."

Bluebird glared defiantly at her tormentor.

"Harper, maybe she can't talk it," Jordan said.

"She can talk."

Harper started whipping the stick across Bluebird's face. Jordan had to turn and look away from the beating when the Indian's cheeks became covered in welts.

"I talk," Bluebird screamed in pain.

"I knew you could talk," Harper said with a laugh as he threw the stick onto the ground. "What happened to Ellis?"

"He beat me. Levi kill him," Bluebird said.

"I never thought that piece of dung had it in him. I guess Levi isn't here to protect you today, though. Where's the money?"

"In cabin at ranch."

"Did you two really think you could get away with killing our cousin and stealing from us? That we wouldn't find you? We followed you to Cheyenne, but you were long gone by then. We just kept heading north. People remember it when they see a white man and an Indian traveling together. Funny thing is that when we got to Fort Laramie, everybody was trying to figure out who the new cowboy and his Indian were at some wedding. If you'd skipped that nonsense, we just might not have found you. They pointed us right here," Harper boasted.

"You bad man," Bluebird said.

"Well, you better get used to bad men, 'cause we're taking you back to Colorado. Me and Jordan are going to share you," Harper said. "Is the ranch straight north of here?"

Bluebird nodded her head. She just wanted to crawl up into a ball and die. The beating had taken the last bit of resistance out of her. She figured that Levi was as good as dead. Her only wish was that maybe they would be together in the afterworld and he would be her man then.

Jordan grabbed Harper by the arm and led him out of hearing distance of Bluebird.

"You shouldn't have worked her over like that," Jordan said.

"Ah, she's just an Indian. She'll heal just fine. By the time we get back to Colorado, she'll be good as new and ready to please."

"Maybe we should take Bluebird and just go. We can't just go riding up there and start ransacking some cabin, trying to find the money. We can always steal more. They'll start looking for her eventually, and we don't know how many of them we may be dealing with. We can kill Levi if he follows us," Jordan said as he looked around as if he were expecting to be caught at any moment.

"We ain't leaving here until Levi is dead. Have you forgotten that he killed Ellis? We owe our cousin that much," Harper said.

"What are we going to do, then?"

"We'll ride up toward the ranch and have a look."

"We can't kill off everyone at that ranch. The whole army in Fort Laramie is liable to track us down if we do," Jordan warned.

"You worry too much. Maybe we can catch Levi off on his own. Let's go have a look," Harper said before walking to his horse.

The outlaws rode to a tree line a couple hundred yards from the ranch house. They hid their horses and took positions behind trees. From their vantage point, they had a clear view of the home and bunkhouse, but the cabin was obscured from their line of vision. They waited there the rest of the morning. Jordan kept hounding Harper to leave, but his brother wouldn't hear of it.

At noon, the crew returned to the ranch for lunch. The outlaws watched a diminutive figure enter the home and four men walk into the bunkhouse.

Levi headed toward the cabin to have lunch with Bluebird. He knew she got lonely during the day, and he liked to eat with her to break up the monotony. As soon as he entered the cabin, a bad feeling came over him. He thought about Bluebird's warning that she thought the Shumans were near the ranch. She was always in the cabin at noon. He looked around and couldn't find anything out of place. Sighing, he tried to figure out what he should do—risk telling Joey and Caleb the truth to get help, or wait and see if Bluebird appeared. The notion that she might be with Claire crossed his mind. He walked over to the house.

Caroline answered his knock.

"Ma'am, is Bluebird in here?"

"No, she isn't. This morning when I left the house to join the rest of you, I saw her walking south, toward the stream, with a bucket. I wondered what she was up to," Caroline replied.

"Okay, thank you."

"Is something wrong, Levi?"

Levi loudly blew out his breath. "I don't know, ma'am. Just seems odd."

As Levi rubbed the back of his neck and looked all about, Caroline decided he looked too troubled for such a seemingly innocent circumstance.

"Please call me Caroline. Levi, is there anything we need to know?"

With shoulders sagging and head down, Levi decided to come clean. His concern for Bluebird overrode his fear of being fired. He could stand losing a job, but not losing Bluebird.

Harper and Jordan watched Levi standing on the porch,

"There's too many of them. We need to just get out of here," Jordan pleaded.

"I think I can kill him from here," Harper said.

"You ain't that good of a shot. Even if you hit him, we'll have the others after us."

"I'm killing Levi. He killed Ellis and gave me this scar on my chin. He's been asking for this for a long time," Harper said as he raised his rifle and took aim at Levi.

The shot hit the porch railing, sending splinters of wood flying through the air toward Levi. He turned toward the sound of the shot. Before he had a chance to see anything, Caroline grabbed his arm and yanked him into the house.

"We can go out the window in the bedroom to get the others," Caroline said.

Claire came running into the parlor. "What is happening?"

"Mother, we have trouble. Just stay in the house," Caroline ordered.

She and Levi scrambled to the back of the house. The shot had interrupted lunch in the bunkhouse, and the men were standing outside trying to figure what was going on when they saw Levi and Caroline crawl out the window.

"Get behind the house," Caroline yelled.

The men came running up to the home.

"What is going on?" Caleb asked.

"We think two men have Bluebird. They just tried to kill Levi. They must be in the cottonwoods by the stream," Caroline answered.

"I told you there was more to their story," Joey lamented.

"Are they good shots?" Caleb asked.

"I don't think so. They're just a couple of outlaws. They aren't particularly bright, and they don't have battle experience. Helpless teamsters are more their style," Levi answered.

"Maybe we should spread out wide and charge them. Five of us should be able to overwhelm them. What do you think, Joey?" Caleb said.

"I suppose so. I don't have any better ideas," Joey replied.

"Six. I'm going, too," Caroline said.

"You don't need to be a part of this," Caleb said.

Caroline, ignoring her husband, marched toward the horses.

"Let's just get this over with," Joey said.

The six riders fanned out so that they could charge from a semicircle.

Jordan started to panic at what he saw. "Let's get Bluebird and make a run for it. We can't hold all of them off."

Harper took one more look at the riders just as they kicked their horses into a gallop. "Let's go," he yelled and began running for their mounts.

Caleb and Joey were in the center of the arc of riders. They saw the outlaws make a break for it. Both noticed that Bluebird was nowhere in sight.

The outlaws' race back to Bluebird proved to be a harrowing ride. Some spots along the stream were strewn with large rocks and boulders. Jordan cut his horse into the water to go around an outcrop, and the animal's feet slipped out from under it. The rider and his mount crashed into the water. Jordan landed on his shoulder and hollered in pain. His mount jumped up and ran off into the pines. Harper saw what happened and yanked his horse to a stop. He pulled his brother up onto the saddle behind him.

Caleb, Joey, and Levi had gained ground on the brothers and could see them up ahead. The brothers' horse was moving slowly under the considerable extra weight. Levi, anxious to put an end to the ordeal, raised his rifle and fired. The shot missed its mark and caused Jordan to look over his shoulder at the advancing riders. He drew his pistol with his good arm and forced himself to hold on with his injured limb. His large frame made it difficult for him to twist his body on the back of the saddle, so his shots went wide.

"Get him," Caleb yelled as they closed to within sixty yards.

The three men fired their rifles almost instantaneously. All three shots found their way into Jordan's back. He flung his arms straight into the air as if making an offering to God before sliding to the ground and bouncing into the water.

Harper decided to make a last stand. He spun his horse around and charged. The riders were now almost on top of him. Harper began firing his revolver as quickly as he could pull back the hammer. A bullet nicked Levi's rib just as their return hail of shots knocked Harper from the saddle and into the water. Levi, ignoring the stinging in his side, jumped from his horse and tackled Harper's arm as the outlaw attempted to raise his gun from a sitting position. He managed to wrest the pistol from the bandit's hand.

"Where's Bluebird?" Levi demanded as Caleb and Joey joined him.

"I'm shot. I need help," Harper said. A bullet had lodged in his thigh and another had hit his chest, high on his right side.

"I mean it—you better tell me where Bluebird is right now. Then we'll help you," Levi yelled as panic began to set in that the brothers may have killed her.

Caroline, Dan, and Reese arrived and ran up to the men.

"No, I'm going to bleed to death. You help me first."

Levi pulled his knife from his belt and slashed it through the air. Harper screamed at the top of his lungs as his left ear fell down his chest. The sight caused Caroline to run behind a tree and begin puking. A full minute passed before the outlaw stopped shrieking.

"If you want to save your other ear, you better start talking fast," Levi warned as he pointed his knife at Harper.

"She's tied to a tree down past where her bucket sits. Jordan is the one that beat her—not me," Harper said, his voice hoarse from screaming.

"I've got to find Bluebird," Levi said as he took off in a sprint.

Caroline returned from behind the tree, looking pale.

Joey glanced over at Caleb and Caroline. "Go with him. The rest of us will watch this one. They might need a woman's touch," he said.

Levi kept shouting Bluebird's name as he ran. By the time he finally heard her call out his name, he was about out of breath and his calf muscle ached something terrible where the snake had bitten him. As Levi burst through the pine branches, he saw Bluebird tied to the tree. The sight stopped him in his tracks. Bluebird's face was nearly unrecognizable from the swelling and welts. Blood oozed from many of the wounds. Her head hung low, as if she had no will to live. She looked up at Levi with glassy eyes that showed no sign of recognition.

He cut the ropes and pulled Bluebird into his lap. The movement caused her to yelp in pain, but she rested her head against Levi's chest. Tears welled up in his eyes as he looked down at her. At that moment, he swore he would take care of her for the rest of his life. She had absorbed a lifetime of abuse, and he would never allow another day of it. He was gently rocking her when Caleb and Caroline found them.

Caroline covered her mouth with her hand and had to look away. She had never seen such a beating in all her life. Her knees felt weak, and she sat down on the ground to collect herself. She tried to be stoic, but found she couldn't control her emotions. Sobs escaped her, and her eyes filled with tears.

Caleb stood over Levi, not knowing what to say.

"Which one of them did this?" Levi asked.

"Harper," Bluebird mumbled through her swollen lips.

"I'm going to take my knife and whittle him to death. Cutting off his ear is just the beginning," Levi swore.

"Let's get her home," Caleb said.

Levi managed to rise from the ground with Caleb's aid while still holding Bluebird. He started walking upstream. Caleb and Caroline followed him.

Caroline couldn't let her conscience remain silent. "Levi, you have every right to kill that man, and I won't blame you if you do. But torture is torture. You'll be keeping company with that devil if you do the same to him."

Levi didn't reply, he just kept walking. When they reached the others, he heard Joey gasp at the sight of Bluebird. Harper was sitting up against a rock, holding a bandana against his chest. Joey had tied another around the outlaw's leg. Levi handed Bluebird to Caleb and drew his pistol.

Harper panicked at the sight of the gun. "I'm telling you that Jordan did that," he protested as Levi aimed the revolver at him.

"You're a liar," Levi said. He inhaled a deep breath and exhaled loudly. Killing another person went against every fiber of his being, but he wanted revenge. Harper didn't qualify as human. Levi pulled the trigger, shooting Harper in the forehead. The outlaw's head flung back violently against the rock, then he slumped over into the stream.

"You three go on and get Bluebird back to the house. Me and the boys will clean up this mess," Joey said.

Levi holstered his gun and turned to take Bluebird.

"You're limping a little. I can carry her for a while," Caleb volunteered.

"No, thank you. She's my responsibility," Levi said as he took the Indian into his arms.

Claire was out in the yard, pacing nervously. When she saw Levi carrying Bluebird, she took one look at the girl and ordered her taken into the house. "Are Joey and the boys okay?" she asked.

"Everybody is fine. We'll catch you up on what happened later," Caroline said.

Caroline directed Levi to the spare bedroom before scurrying off to retrieve fresh water and a cloth. She came back and began bathing Bluebird's wounds. Claire entered the room, carrying butter. She gently smeared the welts with it. Bluebird lay motionless, her eyes closed the whole time. Only her shallow breathing betrayed that she was still living.

Levi got up from the chair where he had been sitting, watching the women. He ran his hand through his hair and finished with a rub of his neck.

"You have a hole in your shirt—and you're bleeding," Caroline said. "Unbutton it and let me see."

"It's nothing," Levi said as he opened his shirt.

He had a two-inch gash on his side. Caroline left the room and returned with iodine and gauze. She applied the medicine and taped on a bandage.

"That should take care of it," Caroline announced.

As Levi buttoned his shirt, he said, "When Bluebird gets better, we will be leaving here. I'm truly sorry to have brought all this upon the ranch. I never thought they'd find us all the way up at Fort Laramie."

Caroline realized she should probably take Levi up on his offer. His lack of forthrightness could have gotten somebody killed. She looked Levi in the eyes as she vacillated about what to do. Glancing over at Bluebird, she got her answer—Bluebird needed a home, and she needed Bluebird to help her face her own fears.

"No. You signed up for a job here, and I mean to hold you to your word. Everybody has some regrets from their past. As long as you stay on the right side of the law, you and Bluebird will have a place to stay."

Chapter 16

The soft moaning from Bluebird awakened Levi. He had spent the night sleeping in a chair in the guest bedroom. After working the kink out of his neck, he moved over to the bed and touched Bluebird's forehead. She felt warm to him, though he'd never taken a person's temperature in his life. He noticed that bruising had set in overnight. Some of the welts had faded somewhat, but others were still raised and angry red, with ooze seeping from them.

"Bluebird."

Bluebird opened her eyes. They looked pained and glazed.

"How are you feeling?" Levi asked.

She didn't respond, but gazed into Levi's eyes as if she were searching for an answer to some question. He wondered if she blamed him for what had happened, but he didn't voice his concern.

Levi poured a glass of water and held it to Bluebird's lips. She greedily drank the glass dry.

"Do you want more?"

She shook her head.

Claire walked into the room in her housecoat. "How is she?"

"I'm not really sure. Her skin seems warm to the touch to me, and she doesn't want to talk," Levi replied.

Reaching down, Claire touched the Indian woman's forehead. Bluebird looked up at Claire with the same expression she had given Levi.

"I think someone better go get Dr. Albright. She definitely has a fever. I was hoping she'd be a little better than this this morning. I'll see if I can get her to eat some breakfast," Claire said.

"Thank you, ma'am. I'm going to head to the cabin and clean up some," Levi said before leaving.

Claire walked to the kitchen and began cooking breakfast. Caroline ambled in with her hand covering her mouth to stifle a yawn and began helping her mother. Caleb and Joey soon joined them. Joey plopped down into a chair. He still felt in an ill mood, thinking about what Levi had confessed to him and Caleb about his past.

"I told Caleb there was more to Levi than he was telling us. I agreed to hire him against my better judgment. I think we should have fired him yesterday when we had the chance," Joey groused.

Caroline turned toward the table. "What is eating you? You, more than anyone else around here, are the one who believes in giving people a new start," she said.

"It took me fifty-two years to get around to getting married, and I guess I'd like to stay that way for a while. I'm getting too old to get shot at," Joey said as he winked at Claire.

"Granted, Levi should have told you about those men coming after him, but do you really think things would have played out any differently yesterday if he had?" Caroline asked.

"Probably not—unless we had been smart enough to send Levi packing immediately. Since when did you become his champion?" Joey asked.

"This may sound crass, but seeing Bluebird in such pain yesterday humanized her for me. I saw her and realized that being an Indian didn't really make her any different from me. We all feel pain and suffering. And she needs a home. Maybe I need her to get over this fear of Indians. I feel an obligation to help them," Caroline answered.

"Well, at least something good might come of it then. I just hope that Levi doesn't fall back into old habits," Joey said.

"It's not like he's the only fugitive around here that we took a chance on hiring," Caroline said, smiling at her husband. "He'll be fine. I just know it."

Claire dumped scrambled eggs into a bowl. "Somebody is going to have to get Dr. Albright. Bluebird isn't as well as I would have expected. I'm going to try to get her to eat as soon as we finish our meal."

"I'll go," Joey said. "Maybe I can ride away some of this crankiness."

After finishing breakfast, Joey saddled his horse and headed to town. The cool morning air had his mount in a frisky mood, so Joey let the animal lope until it slowed down of its own accord. It felt good to be by himself for a change. He relaxed as he took in the scenery for the first time in a long while. After years of living in the West, he sometimes took the mountain views for granted, but today they thrilled him like the first time he ever laid eyes upon them. He made it to town in good time and took a seat in the doctor's office while the physician finished treating a woman with a cough.

"Good day, Dr. Albright," Joey said as the doctor took a seat at his desk.

"Mr. Clemson, I hear congratulations are in order. I must say that I approve of your union with Claire. I like to see two fine people come together. What can I do for you today?" the doctor asked.

"We have an Indian woman on the ranch. A man took a switch to and beat her badly yesterday. She's running a fever today, and is covered in welts. Claire is concerned for her," Joey said.

"I see. How did that happen?"

"It probably would be best for all involved if you didn't know the details. Suffice it to say that that man will never harm her again," Joey said.

The doctor peered over his glasses at Joey a moment before speaking. "As you wish. I'll head to the ranch right now," he said as he began gathering some bottles and salves. He shoved the items into his bag.

Joey's disposition had improved somewhat, but he still wasn't in the mood to work. The previous day's events had gotten him to thinking about how short life is and how a man needed to make the most of the days he had left. Working wasn't high on his list of how to spend those days. He decided to walk to the saloon and have a beer before heading home.

The saloon had just opened for the day, and a few of the town drunks were already sipping their first alcohol of the morning. Paul Myers sat in the back, at the same table he'd been at the first time Joey and Caleb had met him. As Joey waited for the bartender to make his way over, Paul walked toward the bar.

"Bartender, give this man a beer on me," Paul ordered.

Joey nodded his head as a thank-you.

"Why don't you come back to the table? I'd like to have a word with you," Paul said.

Glancing at Paul, Joey noticed his busted lip and bruised jaw and wondered who had put them there. He tried to decide whether he should tell the bounty hunter to go to hell or take him up on the offer in hopes of finding out some information about how much he knew. Choosing the latter, he followed Myers back to the table with beer in hand.

"I'm still waiting on the sheriff in Fort Smith to get back to me. I know your friend is a fugitive. I can just feel it. I was thinking that if you could speed things up and tell me who he is, I'd give you twenty percent of the bounty. I'm sure he killed Frankie, and I plan to even the score. Money has a way of switching loyalties. We'd keep this arrangement to ourselves so you wouldn't have any problems with the new wife and her daughter," Paul said.

Joey took a long sip of beer to give himself time to think. "I don't know any more about Caleb than you do. He just showed up and proved to be a good ranch hand. He's not much for talking. I'll consider your offer, though. Maybe I can get him to tell me about himself now that we're sort of related," Joey said.

"Sounds good to me."

"I have to get home," Joey said before draining the rest of his beer in one long gulp.

Joey mounted up and headed for the ranch. He caught up with the doctor and accompanied him the rest of the way home.

Bluebird had refused to eat. Water was the only thing anybody could get her to accept. Claire had tried to draw some conversation out of her, but the Indian woman was acting as if she was in her own little world—one where she couldn't even hear.

Dr. Albright walked into the bedroom and cursed at the sight before him. "Get me some water and soap, please," he requested.

The doctor took Bluebird's temperature before starting to wash all of her injuries. He tried to talk with her but failed to get any kind of response. After drying her with a towel, he slathered on a salve over her arms, legs, and face. He retrieved a bottle of medicine from his bag and poured it in a spoon.

"Drink this," he said.

Bluebird shook her head.

Dr. Albright had made a study of Indian medicine and knew of willow-bark tea. "This is white man's willow-bark medicine," he said, forcing the spoon into Bluebird's mouth.

The doctor handed Claire the bottle of medicine and the jar of salve.

"A spoonful every four hours. Apply the salve twice a day until the welts are gone," he ordered before nodding his head to suggest going to another room.

Claire led Dr. Albright to the kitchen and poured him a cup of coffee. Caroline and Levi were waiting at the table.

"How is she?" Claire asked.

"She is not well. Her fever is worrisome," the doctor said before taking a sip from the cup.

"Are the wounds infected?" Caroline asked.

"No, the wounds actually look good—if such a thing can be said of injuries. The fever is the result of the trauma her body has suffered. The wounds will heal without any scarring, but I worry about the stress to her body and her mental state. Her mind has clearly shut down. She barely knows what is going on," Dr. Albright said.

"What can we do?" Levi asked.

The doctor took another sip of coffee before speaking. "Kindness—kindness can heal a lot of hurt. Talk to her just as if you're carrying on a conversation, even if she doesn't respond. She's young and strong. I hope she comes around."

Chapter 17

With considerable persuasion, Claire coaxed Levi into going to the cabin to get some rest. His second night spent sleeping in a chair left him looking exhausted, with dark puffy eyes and sagging shoulders. The young man left Bluebird's side just before suppertime. He found the cabin too quiet without Bluebird there to liven it up, though, so he moved to the bunkhouse for the company of Dan and Reese.

Since the doctor's visit the prior day, Bluebird's condition had not changed. The medicine had brought down her temperature some, but the change seemed to have little effect on her well-being. She spent most of her time sleeping and had yet to speak.

After eating supper, Caroline entered the bedroom carrying a tray with a bowl of soup and some bread on it. Bluebird had her head turned, gazing out the window, and did not even bother to look to see who had entered the room.

"I brought you something to eat," Caroline said in a cheerful voice.

Bluebird continued to stare out the window as if nobody was there with her. Caroline set the tray on the nightstand and pulled a chair over from against the wall. She sat down and took hold of Bluebird's hand. Too much had happened in the last couple of days for Caroline to bother with entertaining her fears. While Bluebird still made her feel a little uneasy, even that was fading rapidly—out of necessity.

"Bluebird, you have to eat to get better."

"Why you care?" Bluebird asked as she turned her head to give Caroline an icy look.

"Because I want to see you get better."

"You hate Indians. One less if I die."

"I never said I hate Indians. I said they scare me. There's a big difference. I'm trying to get past that, and I want to get to know you," Caroline said as she took a spoonful of soup and directed it toward Bluebird.

"No," Bluebird uttered before squeezing her lips tightly together like an ill-behaved child.

Caroline dropped the spoon back into the bowl. "I know you don't feel well, but you're going to get better. What happened to you was bad, but you are strong and will get past this."

"I don't belong with white man. I don't belong with Laguna people. I join family in spirit land," Bluebird said.

"You shouldn't talk like that. We are all trying to make this your home," Caroline said.

"Go away," Bluebird ordered before turning to look out the window.

Caroline left the tray and headed to the kitchen. Claire was there, cleaning up after supper. Caleb and Joey sat at the table drinking coffee. Both noticed the briskness of Caroline's step as she entered the room.

"She won't eat for me. She said she wants to join her family in the 'spirit land,' as she called it," Caroline said dejectedly.

Claire untied her apron and tossed it on the table before marching out of the kitchen without saying a word. She entered the bedroom and slammed the door shut, causing Bluebird to jump at the sound and look around to see what was going on. With her hands planted on her hips and feet spread apart, Claire looked as if she were ready to take on any and all comers.

"I will not have talk of going to the spirit world in my house. Everybody on this ranch besides me risked their lives to come to your rescue. You had a horrible thing done to you, but those men are dead. I know you've had a hard life, but that doesn't mean that you can give up. Caroline is trying to get to know you, and you have to give her a chance. Levi is worried sick about you. He probably hasn't figured it out yet, but that man loves you. I can see it in his eyes. Just give him some time. I'm old enough to be your mother, and I'm the big boss on this ranch. I bet your mother made you behave, so I'm making you eat," Claire said before plopping down in the seat.

Bluebird watched with her eyes wide in surprise. Claire had spoken so rapidly that the Indian woman had only understood bits and pieces of the conversation, but she certainly got the gist of it. She had particularly understood the part about mothers ruling the house. She had her mouth open, waiting for the first spoonful, by the time Claire reached for the food. The sight caused Claire to have to stymie a smile.

After Claire administered a few bites, Bluebird said, "I can feed me."

"I know you can, but I'll do it today. You can start tomorrow," Claire said.

"Indians killed Caroline's father and Levi's family. They don't like Indians. I don't belong with white people," Bluebird said.

"You didn't have anything to do with that, and that doesn't mean they don't like you. Levi cares for you, and Caroline is learning to do the same. I don't want to hear any more talk like that. You are staying here. You need to get well and help me around the house. I want to learn some of the things you taught Nils," Claire said before shoveling another spoonful of soup into Bluebird's mouth.

"I'm sorry for trouble."

"You have nothing to be sorry for. You didn't ask for this to happen. I just want you to get better," Claire said.

"My mother like you."

Claire smiled as she handed Bluebird a piece of bread. "I'll take that as a compliment. Sometimes we have to take charge."

After Bluebird swallowed a bite, she said, "Caroline is good. She just scared."

"Yes, she is good. She makes a mother proud. Just give her some time to get used to things. I expect you two will become good friends. You both could use a girl your own age to talk to."

"What is love?" Bluebird asked.

Claire blew out her breath as she tried to think of an answer. "Like Caleb and Caroline getting married. The man you want spend your life with and have babies."

"I love Levi."

Smiling, Claire said, "I know you do. A cabin and nature will take care of the rest."

Bluebird didn't quite understand Claire's last statement, but knew enough to figure out it meant good things.

After finishing her meal, Bluebird said, "I feel better. I wait to go to spirit land."

"Glad to hear that. I think you'll be much better by morning. I need to apply the salve and give you your medicine now," Claire said as she reached for the medicine bottle.

Claire walked back to the kitchen after finishing her application of the salve. She washed her hands. "Bluebird understands the language of mothers just fine. I think she's going to be getting better now. Maybe things can get back to normal around here."

Caleb cleared his throat before speaking. "Claire, I'm not sure what normal is anymore. Frankie Myers's brother is in town. He's a bounty hunter, and he's sure I'm a fugitive. He's trying to find out my history," he said.

The news hit Claire hard. She took a seat at the table. "Are things ever going to get back to the way they used to be around here?" she asked. "I've had about all the excitement I need for a while."

Joey reached over and took Claire's hand. "I'm keeping an eye on things. I went in the saloon yesterday morning, and Paul Myers wanted to have a word with me. He still doesn't know anything."

"Was he sporting some bruises?" Caleb asked.

"Yes, he was. Did you put them there?" Joey asked.

"I did. He got in my face when Caroline and I left the hotel."

"Maybe being left in the dark is better," Claire said.

The four of them exchanged glances with each other, but nobody could think of anything to add to the conversation. They sat in silence until Caroline suggested that she and Caleb go for a walk.

By the next morning, Claire had rebounded from the news of Paul Myers and was back to feeling like her optimistic self. She was the first up. She had just started making breakfast when she heard a knock at the door, interrupting her stirring of pancake batter. She wasn't surprised to find Levi standing on the porch.

"You are certainly getting around early," Claire said.

"I couldn't stop worrying about Bluebird. I had to check on her."

"I don't blame you. I haven't looked in on her yet. Come on in. We'll see about her," Claire said as she led him to the bedroom.

They both were surprised to see Bluebird sitting on the edge of the bed. She even smiled as they entered the room. Her arms, legs, and face were covered in bruises, but the worst of the welts were no longer raised on the skin.

"I'm going back to the kitchen. You two might as well join us for breakfast," Claire said before leaving.

"How are you feeling?" Levi asked as he sat next to Bluebird.

"Much better. I . . . I'm sore all over," Bluebird replied.

"I bet you are. You sure had me scared."

"Claire make me feel better. She like my mother."

An awkward silence followed as Levi tried to think of how to phrase what he wanted to say. He finally gave up on the preparation and took Bluebird's hand into his own. "I care about you, and I like you just the way you are. We need to be together so that I can protect you."

Bluebird sat on the bed. She didn't immediately show any reaction. She thought about what Levi said and tried to make sure she understood what he meant. "You want me to be your squaw?" she asked as she touched her fingers to her chest.

Levi smiled. "I want us to court. You know—be a couple and hold hands and kiss. To see if we're meant for each other."

With a big grin, Bluebird leaned over and kissed Levi on the lips. "Like that?"

"Yes, like that. I think that was a rather good start."

Bluebird felt as if she were on top of the world. She had a hard time believing her mood could change so much since the evening before. Her mind drifted to Claire. She decided that her new mother figure was one of the wise ones who provided guidance to those in need. "I go back to cabin with you," she said.

"I'm ready for you whenever you feel well enough. We better go join the others," Levi said as he stood and helped Bluebird to her feet. They walked into the kitchen holding hands.

Chapter 18

October 12, 1877

The first cold front of the fall hit Fort Laramie with no warning. The day before had been light jacket weather with bright skies and warm temperatures, but overnight ice had formed in buckets and six inches of snow blanketed the ground. Caleb couldn't stop talking about the change in the weather. He put on his heavy coat and walked around the yard like a kid experiencing his first snowfall. Caroline watched him with amusement from a window before deciding to join her husband.

"Let's go for a ride. I want you to see all this before it melts. We can work with the horses when we get back," Caroline said, her breath making wisps of fog.

"That sounds good to me. Seeing the snow beats working on any day," Caleb said.

They saddled Diablo and Buddy before heading north, into the higher elevations. All of the storm clouds had dissipated, and the sky was a deep blue. Sunlight reflected so brightly off the snow that Caleb and Caroline had to squint to see. The wet snow had stuck to the pine trees, bowing the branches with its weight and making a picturesque display of nature. As the sun warmed the air, chunks of snow would occasionally fall from trees and land beside them, making it seem as if the pines were hurling giant snowballs. The farther they rode, the deeper the snow became.

"This is beautiful," Caleb announced.

Caroline looked over at him. His cheeks and ears were rosy, and he needed to wipe a drip from his nose. "Yes, it is. But this isn't all that cold. It will get so bad on some days that it won't be fit to be outside. All this loses some of its luster when you're stuck in the house and trying to keep the fireplaces burning hot enough to stay warm."

"I suppose, but I don't want to think about that today."

"It's a good thing we're married now, or you'd be out of luck for the winter. There's no way I'd put my bare butt in that snow—even for some loving," Caroline said.

Caleb let out a chuckle. "I can raise your temperature so hot that the snow would melt so fast you'd never even feel it."

Caroline grinned, closed her eyes, and shook her head in dismay. "Let's ride up that ridge. That should give you a view," she said as she nudged her horse to start up the slope.

They made it halfway up the incline before the horses began losing their footing and slipping. They dismounted and walked the horses the rest of the way. At the top of the slope, they could see some of the tallest mountains in the area to the north. For the past month, snow had been accumulating at the highest elevations, but now all but the craggiest outcrops of the mountains were carpeted with snow. To complete the view, an eagle floated in the air in search of its next victim.

Caleb let out a whistle. "This must be God's country. I'll never grow tired of looking at the mountains."

"I never have, and I've been looking at them since I could walk," Caroline said.

Using a gloved hand, Caleb swept the snow from two rocks big enough to sit on and pulled a kerchief from his pocket to dry them. The couple sat down and gazed at the mountains without talking.

Finally breaking the silence, Caleb said, "I planned to bring this up when all four of us were together, but now seems as good as a time as any. First off, I want you to know that I think this should be your and Claire's decision. I just want you to think about it . . ." He paused to get Caroline's reaction before continuing.

She let out a sigh that indicated she already knew she wouldn't like his idea before even hearing it. "Go on."

"When Joey and I traveled through Nebraska, we saw the army shutting down Fort Kearney. Once they lick the Indians around these parts, I fear they could do the same thing to Fort Laramie. They may never close the fort for all I know, but they just about have the Indians corralled around here. If that were to happen, the ranch would be hard-pressed to sell enough horses to the area ranchers to make a go of things. I think you should consider adding cattle to the operation. More settlers are coming, and they will need beef to eat more than they will horses to ride," Caleb said.

"And what does Joey think about your idea?" Caroline asked.

"What makes you think I told Joey?"

With a look that warned him not to mess with her, Caroline said, "Because you tell him everything."

"He didn't actually give me his opinion."

Caroline stared off at the mountains. "Daddy would have hated doing that. He didn't like dealing with cattle.

He lived for training horses. They were his true passion."

"I'm not saying to get out of the horse business. You produce too fine of an animal to do that, but I think beef could make a nice supplement to the ranch's income. It's not as if you have to decide anytime soon. You have all winter to think about it," Caleb said.

"Unless we found some bargain prices on cattle from some ranchers . . . If we were to have a harsh winter . . . I've heard of cattle starving and freezing to death in the bad years. We have plenty of good grass here. I do appreciate you thinking about the ranch's future. I'll talk with Mother about it," Caroline said before standing.

They led the horses all the way down the slope before mounting. Caroline followed the trail until she got to two outcroppings of rock. She turned her horse and rode between them until she reached the top of a small valley. A herd of mustangs grazed down below them. The lead mare raised her head and stared up at Caleb and Caroline. The stallion let out a snort before coming up and standing beside the mare while the spring foals pranced around in circles through the snow.

"I never grow tired of seeing those mustangs either," Caleb said.

"I hope you still feel the same way about me in a few years."

"Mountains and horses don't talk back."

"There are a lot of things they don't do that I can do. Keep talking like that, and I'm liable to quit doing some of the things that you're right fond of," Caroline said while bobbing her head in cockiness.

"I think this snow has you as full of yourself as those young foals down there," Caleb said.

"So you say. We'd better get back, or Joey is liable to start sulking."

The couple turned their horses around and headed for home. As they neared a tree line just on the far side of the bunkhouse, Caleb noticed a single set of hoofprints in the snow. He climbed off Diablo and followed them on foot to the trees. Once there, he could also see boot prints.

"Somebody was spying on the house," Caleb announced.

"Where do you think the tracks go from here?"

"It looks like they follow the trees going west, heading back the way they came," Caleb replied.

"Do you think it was the Myers brother?"

"I wouldn't be surprised. I don't know why he decided to do it the snow. I wonder if he's found out something and is making a plan," Caleb said.

"Let's see if we can catch him," Caroline said. She heeled her horse into a trot, leaving Caleb.

Caleb scrambled onto his horse and took off after his wife, fearing what could transpire if she surprised Paul Myers.

"That wasn't funny," Caleb said when he caught up with her.

"It will be a lot less funny if I catch him. I'll not have some lowlife bounty hunter ruin our life together," Caroline said as she kicked her horse into a lope.

"Caroline, slow down. You're going to wear the horses out in this snow—if they don't slip and break a leg first," Caleb hollered.

She pulled her horse to a stop before turning the animal around. "We need to find a solution to this problem. Waiting for him to make the first move is pure folly."

"What are we supposed to do—just go out and murder him?" Caleb asked.

"I guess that depends on if you value his life or your own more. We're not talking about a pillar of the community. A bounty hunter is only about two notches above most of the filth they track down," Caroline said defiantly.

"That's a slippery slope to head down."

"Is it? How much different is it than you killing Nathan after he tried to have me killed? Paul Myers is after revenge more than anything. A bounty is just his excuse," Caroline said.

"You have a fair point."

"I certainly do. And we are not telling Mother about this," Caroline said.

They rode back to the barn and put up their horses. After that, they joined the others in the pasture to spend the rest of day working at training horses to change gaits on cue. By the time supper neared, everybody felt tired and cold from a long afternoon.

Claire had three hot brandy toddies ready when Joey, Caleb, and Caroline walked into the house. Caleb and Joey sat down at the kitchen table and sipped their drinks while Caroline stood in front of the fireplace warming her numb hands.

"You all look frozen," Claire said.

"It's not that it's very cold, but the body needs time to adjust to the change in weather. There sure wasn't any easing into this," Joey said as he cupped the glass to warm his hands.

"I made stew. I thought that would warm up everybody," Claire announced.

Caroline joined the men at the table. Claire noticed her daughter's unusually quiet demeanor.

"What's wrong with you? Did you have a bad day?" Claire asked.

"No, I'm just cold. I'll be fine when I warm up," Caroline said, trying to sound chipper. She avoided making eye contact, but she could sense Joey and her mother looking at her. She assumed they knew she was lying.

"Well, drink down that toddy. It's good for whatever ails you," Claire said.

Chapter 19

October 14, 1877

The snow and cold weather disappeared as fast as they had come, leaving the ground soft and spongy. Joey decided that training the horses would tear the pasture up too much, so he decided to have the men work on the odd jobs that needed tending to around the ranch. He knew that Levi was itching to make a trip to town and decided to send the young man to get some supplies on the buckboard wagon. Joey had put his reservations about Levi to the side, figuring that he might as well trust him until he saw a reason to do otherwise. And truth be told, Levi was hard not to like. The young man was certainly earnest in his attempts to learn ranching and showed signs of having a keen mind and an amiable personality.

"We need six bags of oats from Chester's feed store, and Caroline has a list of things to get at Bell's Dry Goods and Mike's General Store. She usually goes, but I told her that you needed to make a trip to town. I hope she won't be out of sorts about it, but she is a woman after all," Joey said with a grin.

"Thank you, Joey. I really do appreciate this," Levi said.

"Be careful. Tell them to put it on the Langley tab," Joey said.

Levi started to leave, then turned back toward Joey. "Hey Joey, can I ask you a question?"

"You can ask anything you like, but it don't mean I'll have an answer."

"Do you think it matters that Bluebird is an Indian?" Levi asked.

"How so?"

"You know, like if I were ever to think about marrying her."

Joey rubbed his chin and scrunched his face as he contemplated an answer. "Of course it does—providing it matters to you. If you are going to go through life thinking that you settled for an Indian when you should have married a white girl, then that's a problem. You'll eventually grow bitter about your union. But if you don't give a damn about what anybody else thinks, and she's the one that makes your heart sing and makes you be the best person that you can be, well, that's a horse of a different color."

Levi smiled. "Thank you, Joey. I think I needed to hear that," he said before going.

After retrieving the list from Caroline—without any signs she minded him making the trip instead of her— Levi hitched up the wagon. Bluebird joined him in the shed. She had gotten past most of her soreness, but she still looked pitiful since more of her skin was covered in bruises than not. He hastily helped her up onto the seat so that they could set off for town.

Levi was down to two changes of clothes. Bluebird had destroyed one pair of his pants by slitting them when the snake bit him, and he had ruined a shirt when he got shot rescuing her from the Shumans. Her clothing situation was even worse. The only things she had decent to wear were her deerskin dress and two dresses that Caroline had given her. Bluebird was even smaller than Caroline, and the dresses hung on her like hand-me-downs from a big sister. Levi felt excited to get to town to buy Bluebird clothes with his own earnings. He wouldn't have to touch the loot she had taken from the hideout. He guessed Claire must have figured out that he might be low on money, because she had advanced him his first month of pay without him even asking.

"The weather sure is pretty. It's hard to believe we don't even need jackets after all that snow," Levi said, realizing his attempt at conversation sounded about as interesting as watching paint dry.

"Yes, weather nice," Bluebird replied.

Since deciding to court, the two had found their relationship to be in unfamiliar territory. It felt awkward. Neither had ever romanced another person. Levi's knowledge of women went no farther than whores in brothels. All of the men in Bluebird's past had forced themselves upon her after she had been kidnapped and really counted as rapists. Instead of proceeding from where their relationship had evolved, they both acted as if they were practically strangers. Also looming large was the fact that they lived together. The sexual tension only exasperated their predicament and made them even more self-conscious.

"I'm going to buy you two of the prettiest dresses in the store," Levi boasted.

"I never had new dress from store."

"Well, it's about time that you do. I think better days are ahead. We don't have the Shumans to worry about, and we couldn't have found better people to work for if we tried."

"All of them very good to us. Claire makes me feel like—her daughter," Bluebird said.

"Even Reese is minding his manners since seeing us hold hands," Levi added.

Bluebird grinned. "You are a jealous man."

Levi let out a laugh. "You remembered the word. Maybe I am. I've never been in the company of such a pretty girl before now."

Having gotten past struggling for something to say, they talked and laughed the rest of the way to town. Levi was anxious to buy Bluebird the dresses. He made his first stop the dry goods store. He grinned when they reached their destination and quickly jumped from the seat.

"This is where they have the dresses," Levi said as he helped Bluebird down from the buckboard.

He opened the door for her and followed her into the store. Mr. Bell stood behind the counter talking to some soldiers. The merchant was a short, pudgy man in his sixties with his hair combed to cover his balding head. He eyed Levi and Bluebird as they passed by the counter.

"We don't allow Indians in this store," Mr. Bell said.

"What?" Levi asked.

"You heard me. I don't allow savages to sully my establishment. Now get," the merchant ordered.

"I'm here to buy her some dresses. I have the money in my pocket," Levi protested.

"Not in my store. I don't need your money."

"You heard the man," one of the soldiers said.

"This isn't any of your concern. Mind your own business," Levi warned the soldier.

Without warning, the soldier sucker punched Levi in the temple. As Levi's knees buckled, two of the other soldiers jumped him. They pummeled Levi with a fury of punches to the head and stomach while the soldier that had done the talking added a couple of kicks. Levi was defenseless against the onslaught. He curled up into a ball for protection. Bluebird grabbed the collar of one the soldiers to pull him off Levi and got backhanded into a shelf. Once the men had beaten Levi into submission, they dragged him out of the store and down the street.

"Injun, you better get out of here, or I'll put more bruises on you than you already have. I'll drag your red ass down to the stockade to join that Injun-loving man of yours," Mr. Bell threatened.

Bluebird ran out of the store and stopped in front of the wagon. She looked down the street and saw the men still dragging Levi away. Her mind raced as she tried to decide what to do. She didn't know whether to follow the soldiers or head back to the ranch. Figuring she had no choice but to get help, Bluebird decided to return to the ranch. She had never driven a wagon before and nervously climbed onto the seat. After a couple of failed attempts, she managed to release the brake. Pausing to remember what she'd seen others do, she lightly popped the reins and then worked them sort of like she did when horseback riding. To her surprise, the team of horses made a U-turn in the street. She traveled slowly out of town, but once she got comfortable steering the wagon, she popped the whip until the horses took off in a brisk gait.

Returning to the ranch seemed as if it took forever. Bluebird worried the whole way that the soldiers were taking Levi off to kill him. She wanted desperately to talk to Claire. The wise one would know what to do. Bluebird stopped the wagon in the yard, dashed onto the porch, and pounded on the door. She had arrived at lunchtime. Caleb greeted her.

"Bluebird, how was your trip to town?" Caleb asked, not noticing she looked stressed or realizing that she had arrived home too soon.

"I need to see Claire. Something bad," Bluebird said.

"Everybody get in here. Something is wrong," Caleb bellowed as he led Bluebird inside the parlor.

"What is it, Bluebird?" Claire asked.

The sight of Claire caused Bluebird to let out a cry. Her shoulders began trembling.

"Soldiers take Levi. I don't know where," Bluebird said between sobs.

Claire realized she needed to comfort Bluebird before she would be able to find out any useful information. She hugged the Indian woman and patted her back until the crying slowed.

"Okay, Bluebird, tell me everything that happened," Claire said as she took a step back.

"We go in store and man says no Indians. Levi argue with him."

"Which store?" Caroline interrupted.

"One with dresses," Bluebird replied. "Then soldier argue with Levi. Three soldiers beat him and drag him away. Store man tell me to leave or I go to stock ... something."

"Stockade," Joey said.

"Yes."

"I didn't know that Mr. Bell felt like that," Caroline noted.

"Caleb and I can ride to town and get this straightened out," Joey said as he began moving toward the door.

Claire held her hand up to stop her husband. "No, Bluebird and I will go to town to fix this. I plan to pay Cedric Bell a visit and then go see Captain Willis. Cedric will make this right, or I'll see to it that he loses so much business that he has to close his doors."

"Are you sure you don't need some help?" Joey asked.

Shaking her head, Claire sighed. "Believe me—I can take care of this." She darted back to the kitchen and returned with two ham sandwiches, handing one to Bluebird before shepherding her out the door.

"Will they kill Levi?" Bluebird asked as they headed down the driveway.

"No, a stockade is like a jail. We'll get him out of there. Quit your worrying. Everything will be fine," Claire assured her.

"I make trouble all the time."

"You didn't cause this. Mr. Bell did. He might have started it, but I'm going to finish it," Claire promised.

They traveled down the road in silence, eating their sandwiches.

"You good to me," Bluebird said after swallowing her last bite of pork.

Claire put her arm around Bluebird. "I just like everybody to be happy. I want to see you and Levi get a fair shake in life."

By the time they reached Fort Laramie, Claire had herself worked up and ready to pounce. She halted the wagon in front of the dry goods store and led the way through the door.

"Good afternoon, Mrs. Langley," Mr. Bell said, his view of Bluebird blocked by Claire's body.

"It's Mrs. Clemson now," Claire said as she moved to the side and put her arm around Bluebird. "This is Bluebird. She works for me and so does Levi, that cowboy you argued with today."

Mr. Bell lifted his elbows off the counter and stood up straight. "I have a policy. No Indians allowed," he said, pointing at a handwritten sign that he had put up after the incident earlier that very day.

Claire walked over to the sign and ripped it down. She crumbled the paper and tossed it on the floor. "Your policy changes as of today."

"You have no right to tell me what I can and cannot do," he protested.

"Cedric, I've always favored your store over O'Malley's, but that could change today. And if it does, I'll visit every ranch wife in riding distance and encourage her to do the same. You know I have the clout to do it. My late husband, Jackson, was good friends with Captain Willis. I'm sure if I asked him, he'd be more than happy to suggest that his soldiers frequent the other dry goods store, too. Do I make myself clear?"

Cedric eyed Claire with a look of pure malevolence. "Yes, I guess you do."

"Good, now Bluebird and I are going to pick out a couple of dresses for her, and then the three of us are going to pay Captain Willis a visit. You are going to make him understand that today was just a little misunderstanding and that his soldiers overreacted. Can you do that, Mr. Bell?"

"Whatever you like," Cedric said disgustedly.

Claire led Bluebird to the back of the store where the dresses were located. Bluebird found a bright blue dress and another red one that she liked. Claire held them up to Bluebird and decided they would fit.

"You will look beautiful in them. Levi will be smitten," Claire announced.

"Thank you, Claire, for all your help," Bluebird said.

Waving her hand through the air, Claire acted as if what she had done was nothing. She returned to the front of the store carrying the clothing. "Wrap these and put them on my tab."

Mr. Bell carefully folded the dresses and wrapped them in brown paper. He neatly tied the bundle and handed it to Claire. "I'm ready," he said.

The three of them walked briskly to the fort and entered Captain Willis's office. The captain's private office door was shut. The captain's aide greeted them.

"What can I do for you all?" the aide asked.

"I'd like to see Captain Willis," Claire said.

"The captain is not taking any appointments today."

"Could you make an exception? He knows me well, and I really need to speak to him," Claire said.

"I'm sorry, ma'am. I'm just following orders," the aide said.

The door opened, and Captain Willis stepped into the room. "Mrs. Langley—or rather Mrs. Clemson—I thought I recognized your voice. Congratulations on your marriage. Joey is a fine man. What can I do for you?"

"Mr. Bell has something he needs to tell you," Claire said.

Mr. Bell cleared his throat and patted the hair combed over his bald spot. "I had a little disagreement with one of Mrs. Clemson's ranch hands today. Three soldiers intervened when it wasn't really necessary and dragged the ranch hand to the stockade. I came here to ask you to release him. It really was just a little misunderstanding."

Captain Willis looked at Claire and then toward Mr. Bell. He had no idea what exactly was going on, but he did know Claire had her thumb on Cedric Bell and was squishing the daylights out of him because of whatever it was. "Very well. Let's go get him."

"Levi Bolander is his name," Claire said.

The captain led the group to the stockade. "A man by the name of Levi Bolander was brought in here today. I want him released immediately," the captain ordered.

The guard left the room and returned in short order with Levi. Levi sported a black eye and a bruised cheek, but otherwise seemed to be in good shape. The guard handed him his hat and gun belt.

"Tell everyone at the ranch that I say hello," Captain Willis said before taking his leave.

Mr. Bell bolted for the door a moment later.

"Let's get you home," Claire said.

"Thank you, ma'am."

As they walked back to the wagon, Bluebird asked, "Are you hurt?"

Levi let out a little snicker. "Compared to the licking you took, that was nothing. My pride is hurt more than anything. I didn't make much of a stand," he said.

"They jump you. You had no chance," Bluebird said in his defense.

As they were returning home, Levi said, "I bet you rue the day that Bluebird and I showed up at the ranch."

Claire gave a small smile. "No, not at all. I certainly wish things could have gone better, but that's the way life goes sometimes. Bluebird is going to be good for Caroline, and you are good for the ranch. We can always use another sharp mind. I like you both."

They arrived back at the ranch to find Joey, Caleb, and Caroline on the porch. Only Dan and Reese had gotten any real work done that day. The other three had fretted the afternoon away, worrying about what was going on in town. They hustled out and met the wagon.

"Looks like you accomplished what you set out to do," Joey said.

"You better believe I did. Cedric Bell best remember what I told him," Claire said proudly.

"I'll put up the wagon and horses," Levi said, wanting to be alone.

Joey helped Claire down from the wagon. Levi drove the team to the shed to unhitch the horses. He wasn't in the mood to talk and worked in silence. After putting the horses in the barn, he and Bluebird walked to the cabin. Levi dropped onto his cot and didn't talk.

"Do you want to see my new dresses?" Bluebird asked excitedly.

The mention of the dresses only further reminded Levi of what a disaster the day had been. He had really wanted to be the one to buy her new clothes. "Yeah, sure."

Bluebird stepped behind a privacy partition that they had rigged up. She stepped out a few moments later, smiling in her new blue dress. "See?" she said as she pulled the full skirt out to the sides.

"You look real nice," Levi said without much enthusiasm.

Not noticing his lackluster response, Bluebird scurried behind the partition and soon emerged in her red dress.

"That looks good, too. I like the blue one the best." Levi chuckled at the thought that a girl named Bluebird looked best in a blue dress.

Bluebird changed back into her deerskin outfit and emerged to find Levi snoring softly. While he slept, she sat at the table, looking out the window and wondering where life would next lead her. After escaping Ellis and the hideout, she had hoped life would become easier, but it seemed as if she had just taken a tumble down a hill and had yet to reach the bottom. She remained sitting until it was time to go to the bunkhouse and start supper. By the time she was ready to put the food on the table for Dan and Reese, Levi had joined them. The two ranch hands could see from Levi's dour expression that he wasn't in any mood to talk, so they ate their meals in silence. After the dishes were washed, Levi and Bluebird made a quick departure for the cabin.

Levi plopped into a chair at the table. "Bluebird, I'm sorry about today. I so wanted to buy you those dresses and make you feel special. I made a mess of things," he said.

Bluebird sat down across from him. "You are not to blame. You did your best."

"Well, my best must not be very good then."

She reached out and touched his hand. "You too hard on you," she said.

Levi smiled at her English but didn't have the heart to correct her. "Do you think you would be better off if you were still with Ellis? Maybe I should have left well enough alone."

Pulling her hand back, Bluebird thought about Claire's fearlessness that day. "I won't listen to that talk. I'm happy now. Bad days now not as bad as bad days with Ellis. Stop it," she demanded.

With his eyes meeting Bluebird's gaze, Levi attempted a smile that mostly failed. As he looked at the bruises on Bluebird's face, he decided that too many misfortunes had happened in too of a short time to leave him feeling anything but depressed. Today's failure had been like an exclamation point on all that had gone wrong lately. He was also very aware that since declaring his intention to court Bluebird he had been stumbling around like a drunk in a dark alley with no idea how to proceed. He glanced out the window as dusk settled in, wishing darkness would hurry up and come so he could go to bed.

"Let's work on alphabet," Bluebird said as she lit the oil lamp.

Levi had come up with the idea to teach Bluebird how to read. She had enthusiastically agreed to the proposition. Each night, he would go through all the letters with her, working on the sounds of each and then finishing things off with having her sound out some simple words.

"Okay, if you want to," he said quietly.

They worked on sounding out the letters for better than an hour. Levi didn't mind. He liked teaching Bluebird, and she was proving to be a quick learner. The task also kept him from thinking about how low he felt.

By the time they finished with her reading a few words aloud, darkness had set in. Levi looked out the window and said, "I'm going to go to bed. Tomorrow has to be better."

"It's been a long day," Bluebird responded.

They prepared for bed in silence. After Levi plopped down on his cot, Bluebird blew out the lamp and dropped onto her bed. As the minutes passed by, the silence in the pitch-black room became palpable. Even their breathing was so shallow as to be noiseless. Levi stared up into the darkness, knowing that sleep would be a long time in coming. He felt so wound up that his skin seemed tingly.

The stillness was finally interrupted by the sounds of Bluebird stirring. Levi listened intently, wondering what she might be doing. He could hear her walking his direction and then felt his cover being slowly pulled back. Her warm, naked body covered him, and her mouth found his lips.

Chapter 20

Pins and needles sensations shot through Levi's hand and roused him from his sleep. He opened his eyes to see Bluebird's head resting on his arm. The sight of her brought a smile to his face and made him hesitant to try and relieve his discomfort. They had spent the night squeezed together on his cot. He studied Bluebird's face as she slept. She seemed to be smiling, and he hoped she dreamed of him. He felt like shouting at the top of his lungs to the world that he was in love. The previous night had been a revelation in the difference between having sex and making love. He tried to think of an analogy and snickered when he came up with the sorry example of the difference between seeing an apple pie and tasting one. As he tried to free his arm, Bluebird woke.

"Hello there," Levi said.

Bluebird stretched her neck and kissed Levi on the lips. "Hello."

"I love you," he said. In his newly found state of bliss, the words popped out unintentionally. The smile Bluebird gave him might have been the best moment of his life.

"I love you," she replied.

They wasted little time in making love again with the desperation of two people who had spent years without knowing the feeling. Afterward, Levi had to throw on his clothes and run out of the cabin without breakfast to avoid being late for work. As he jogged toward the bunkhouse, he suddenly felt the soreness from the beating he'd taken—something he hadn't noticed at all while in bed with Bluebird. Stifling a grin as he caught up with Joey walking over from the house, Levi decided he'd need more of the same distraction from his aching body as soon as possible.

"You have a lot of giddyup in your step for a man that took a beating," Joey observed.

"I just wanted to be ready to work first thing this morning. I caused enough trouble yesterday to last awhile. I don't want to add to the reasons you probably already regret bringing us here," Levi said.

"So you say," Joey said with a quizzical expression as he observed the young man's jaunty step.

Dan and Reese joined the two men outside as Joey waited for Caleb and Caroline to arrive. The couple emerged from the house a couple of minutes later.

"How are you feeling?" Caroline asked Levi.

"Oh I'm fine. I've felt a lot worse after a fall from a horse," Levi answered.

"Has Bluebird calmed down any? She was so worried about you," Caroline said.

"She is fine. That girl is a tough one."

"I think I'll check on her, if you boys would be so kind as to saddle Buddy for me," Caroline said.

Levi, unable to make eye contact, looked down at his boots before speaking. "Ma'am, I don't really think you have to do that. I don't want to burden you. She seemed like her usual self this morning to me."

"I don't mind," Caroline said as she started walking toward the cabin.

She truly felt concerned for Bluebird. The young Indian woman had been through an awful lot of trauma in such a short time. Caroline also had an ulterior motive. She no longer feared Bluebird and had even grown fond of her, but in irrational moments, she could sense her anxiety toward Indians creeping back into her mind. She had no intention of ceding the progress she had made.

Bluebird quickly came to the door after hearing the knock. "Caroline. Good morning."

"Good morning, Bluebird. I thought I would see how you were feeling this morning," Caroline said.

"Come in. I feel good."

Caroline stepped inside and immediately noticed the bacon just starting to sizzle in the frying pan. Her face betrayed her surprise. Bluebird noticed the facial expression and glanced over her shoulder to see where Caroline was looking.

"Levi missed breakfast. I'm fixing food for me," Bluebird explained.

"Oh. That's too bad."

Bluebird couldn't contain her grin. "Levi love me. Missed meal for love," she said.

The smile on Bluebird's face was so radiant that it seemed to light the room and proved so contagious that Caroline let out a squeal. In her exuberance, she hugged Bluebird. Bluebird stood stiff as a board for a moment from the surprising development before returning the embrace.

"I'm so happy for you. I knew he would come around," Caroline said.

Grinning sheepishly, Bluebird said, "I help him come around."

Caroline let out a giggle. "Good for you. Sometimes you have to lead a horse to water and a man to his— heart. I have to go. See you later."

After lunch, Bluebird found herself giddy over the turn of events between her and Levi. She couldn't find anything to do to keep her mind occupied, so she walked to the house and knocked.

"Bluebird. Is something wrong?" Claire asked as she answered the door.

"No, just wanted to thank you again for yesterday," Bluebird answered.

Claire studied the young woman a moment. She could see that Bluebird was in a fidgety state, shifting her weight from one foot to the other and rubbing her hands together. "You are very welcome. Come in. We can have some coffee."

"Okay."

"Do you like coffee?" Claire asked as she led Bluebird to the kitchen.

"Yes, with sugar."

"Me too. Have a seat," Claire said as she started making a fresh pot.

"Levi loves me," Bluebird blurted out.

Claire turned toward the table. "Well, it's about time he figured that out. Men can be a little slow sometimes. Congratulations."

Bluebird grinned. "I told Caroline. She hugged me. I don't scare her now."

"I'm happy to hear that, too. I knew she would come around. I guess today is a whole lot better than yesterday," Claire said as she poured the water into the pot.

"At the hideout, Levi had cold heart. He never talk to me. He has changed much."

"I think men are either good or bad. Sometimes the good ones lose their way, and if they are lucky, they find their way back to being good," Claire said.

"What is a lawyer?" Bluebird asked.

Claire turned and scratched her head absentmindedly as she tried to think about how to answer the question. "He helps people settle fights over land or horses or to stay out of jail. Things like that."

"Like elder in council."

"Yes, I would imagine so. Why do you ask?"

"Levi wanted to be lawyer when he was boy," Bluebird answered.

"Really? I bet he likes to read. I'll have to show him our library. I think Jackson even had a couple of law books in there."

"Jackson was Caroline's father?" Bluebird asked.

"Yes."

"Indians kill him. Why do you not hate Indians?"

"I had a brother that died fighting for the Union in the war. If I hated all Southerners, I would have to hate Caleb. I can't hate all Indians because a Crow war party killed Jackson. We knew it would be dangerous when we moved here. All of us ranchers were fighting the Indians for the land," Claire answered.

Bluebird didn't understand everything that Claire had said, but she understood her meaning. "I'm happy you like me."

"Me too."

Bluebird didn't leave until it was time to make supper. The afternoon had flown by for both of them. Claire talked a lot about the ranch's early days and then questioned Bluebird on a variety of things concerning Indian cooking and crafts. Bluebird had explained in as much detail as her English would allow all the intricacies that went into making pottery and deerskin clothing. They parted with a deepening friendship and a new appreciation of each other's earlier life.

After supper, Levi felt compelled to spend some time with Dan and Reese for fear of alienating the two cowboys if he and Bluebird again made a quick exit. The two ranch hands were already growing bored with each other's company since Joey and Caleb had deserted them for wives and life in the house. Levi played dominoes with them while Bluebird watched over his shoulder to learn the game. As darkness set in, Levi excused himself on the pretense of being tired. He and Bluebird all but skipped back to the cabin.

"I missed you today," Levi said as he lit the oil lamp.

"You missed breakfast," Bluebird said with a smile.

Levi let out a chuckle. "Yes, I did, but only my belly complained."

"I missed you, too."

"I didn't think today was ever going to end," Levi said as he took a seat.

"I go see Claire today. Make day go fast. We had nice long talk," Bluebird said as she joined Levi at the table.

"Really? What did you talk about?"

"Everything. She has many books you can read," Bluebird said.

"Books? How did that come up in conversation?"

"I tell her you wanted to be a lawyer when boy."

Levi leaned back in his chair. He pursed his lips and ran his hands through his hair. "Did she laugh at me?" he asked.

"No. No, you silly. She might have . . . law books for you to read," she said.

"Oh. I guess I was being silly. She must think I am intelligent then. I'm afraid I lost most of those smarts through the years," Levi said, grinning sheepishly.

Bluebird got up from her chair and walked around the table. She sat down in Levi's lap and wrapped her hands around his neck. "Everybody good to us. We need to make them proud. You teach me letters now," she said.

"Right now?"

"Yes, work first. That the Indian way," Bluebird said before giving Levi a kiss.

"You better be a quick learner tonight then," Levi said and gave Bluebird a wink.

Chapter 21

Claire and Caroline sat at the kitchen table ripping the stitching from a dress. Now that Bluebird had the two store-bought dresses to wear, Claire had made it a mission to alter the outfits that Caroline had given the Indian woman so that they fit properly.

"I think buying Bluebird a couple more dresses would be money well spent rather than go to all this trouble," Caroline said as she rubbed a finger that she had pricked.

"Caroline, you weren't raised to be wasteful. You don't have anything better to do this evening anyway," Claire said.

Joey and Caleb were also sitting in the kitchen, reading books. Caleb looked up when he heard Claire's comment and rolled his eyes. Caroline had to stifle a smile. She had watched him fidget all night, and knew what he had on his mind. Thankfully, two couples living under one roof hadn't proved to be much of an issue. With their bedrooms on opposite sides of the house, the newlyweds had managed to have their privacy.

"Levi and Bluebird make such a cute couple. I'm so happy for them. And Bluebird is such a delight to be around. Bringing them onto the ranch was the right thing to do," Claire said.

"I think she and I are going to be friends. I really to do like her," Caroline said.

"And to think of all the fussing you did when they first showed up here," Claire reminded her daughter.

Caroline shook her head in dismay at her mother's need to remind her of past mistakes. She decided to bring up the subject of acquiring cattle in hopes the topic would bring an end to dress alterations.

"Caleb thinks we should consider expanding into cattle in case they ever shutter the fort," Caroline said to her mother.

"Oh really? Jackson would have hated that idea back in the day," Claire said.

"So you think it's a bad idea then?"

"I never said any such thing. Your daddy, if he was anything, was adaptable. As we are all well aware, he died before the Indians were defeated. Jackson most surely would have gotten into cattle if it meant survival of the ranch," Claire said as she ripped out the last thread connecting a sleeve to a shoulder.

"What do you think about cattle, Joey?" Caroline asked.

Joey looked up from his book. "Caleb and I decided that it should be your and Claire's decision."

"If that isn't just like a man. They can give you their opinion on everything under the sun whether you ask for it or not, but the moment that you want their input, they go all mealymouthed," Caroline accused.

Joey let out a little chortle as he grinned at Caroline. "You would hurt my feelings if I didn't know you loved me. Maybe I think you don't have a clue as to when you need advice," he said, clearly enjoying the bickering.

"Joseph Clemson, tell us what you think," Claire demanded.

"Uh oh. I know what it means when my full name gets used. I better talk before my middle name gets added in there," Joey said with a wink at his wife. "I think the idea is worth considering. We really have more cowboys than we do work right now, and cattle would solve that problem. I would start out small, maybe a hundred head until we get up to speed."

Caleb looked over at Joey and grinned. "Maybe we can round up all of Nathan Horn's cattle and rebrand them. By now, they are probably scattered all over half of the Wyoming Territory," he said to add to the mischief.

Caroline stiffened her posture. "Caleb, that is not funny. Most of the ranchers around here have a pretty good idea that you and Joey killed Nathan."

"Our wives seem to lack a sense of humor tonight. We might have to go out in the barn and talk to our horses," Joey teased.

"You're liable to be out in that barn sleeping with your horse if you're not careful," Claire said. She nodded her head with authority. "All joking aside, Nelly Nixon told me at church Sunday that Nathan's sister was tracked down in Kansas. She is staying here, at Nathan's house, while she settles the estate. Maybe I could approach her about buying some of the herd. Caroline and I can talk about it some more since our men are running to cover their backsides in case this all turns out be more manure than beef."

"I've already decided that we should look into it—if you don't object," Caroline said to her mother.

"Good. We'll go in the morning to talk to Nathan's sister. Now get back to pulling out stitching. I figured out your trick of using conversation to get out of work back when you were about seven years old."

"Mother, you can be so bossy."

Caleb unintentionally let out a sigh.

Putting her hands on her hips, Claire said, "Young man, the night is still young. There's still plenty of time left for you to dash off to that bedroom with Caroline."

Turning red, Caleb looked down at his book. The others burst into fits of giggles.

The following morning, Caleb harnessed the buggy and drove it into the yard. Claire and Caroline met him in front of the house. Both women had covered their shoulders in shawls to ward off the cool morning. Caroline had decided to wear a dress for the occasion. Caleb, admiring the beauty of his wife as he helped her into the carriage, covertly gave her a pinch on the butt.

"Wish us luck," Caroline said, ignoring her husband's playfulness.

"Yeah, I wonder what Nathan's sister has heard about what happened. She might not be friendly," Caleb said.

"All she can do is run us off the property," Claire said as she took Caleb's hand for support as she climbed onto the seat.

"See you soon," Caroline said before popping the reins and leaving.

Neither woman had been to the Horn ranch since the killings. The appearance of the place took them by surprise. The yard was overgrown from a summer of neglect, and the bunkhouse still sat in a state of disrepair—Caleb had used dynamite to blow up one end of the structure. An additional seven graves filled the family cemetery and made for an uncomfortable sight.

The women waded through the tall grass, and Caroline knocked on the door. A woman of about Claire's age greeted them. She wore a plain dress and had her hair in a tight bun. Years of working in the sun had aged her skin beyond her years.

"May I help you?" the lady asked.

"Hi, I'm Claire. This is my daughter, Caroline. We're from the Langley ranch. May we have a moment of your time?"

The woman eyed them with a look of puzzlement. "I'm Lena Welsh. Come on in."

Lena led them into the parlor. A spot on the floor showed the unmistakable stain of blood left there for too long, and bullet holes in the wall marked the location where Nathan Horn had died. Caroline and Claire tried not to be obvious about averting their eyes from the sights.

"You're from the ranch that Nathan picked a fight with. And you must be the young woman that he tried to kill. I've been informed about all that went on here," Lena said in a straightforward tone.

Claire was taken aback by the woman's brashness. She hesitated a moment while she carefully chose her words. "Yes, we are. I tried to reason with Nathan to get him to come to his senses, but he wouldn't listen. He was out to ruin our livelihood."

"So you killed him," Lena said matter-of-factly.

"Ma'am, we had nothing to do with that," Claire protested.

"But I bet you know who did. It doesn't make a difference anyway," Lena said. She waved her hand through the air as if she were swatting away her accusation. "Nathan and I hadn't spoken in years, and I hadn't seen my nephew, Milo, since he was a small boy. When my parents died, Nathan cheated me out of my share of the inheritance. That's where he got the money to come out West and build his ranch. I know full well what Nathan was capable of doing. I guess I'm getting my inheritance now. You reap what you sow. Now, what brings you ladies out here?"

"We wanted to see if you were interested in selling some of the cattle," Claire stated.

Lena let out a little chortle. "I've yet to figure out the size of his herd. Nathan wasn't much on keeping records, as far as I can tell."

"He always claimed he had five hundred head," Caroline said.

"And how many head do you want?"

"We want a hundred head of cattle and three bulls."

"I don't know anything about cattle prices. We're farmers in Kansas. What would be a fair price?" Lena asked.

"My husband says that cows go for twenty-five dollars a head and bulls go for ninety," Claire answered.

"Since I have no earthly idea how I'm going to take care of all this, that sounds like a fair deal to me. I'll take you at your word. Your men can round up whichever ones you choose. I'll mention in the bill of sale that any double-branded cattle are yours," Lena said.

"Thank you, Mrs. Welsh. I'll get you a bank draft. You might also pay a visit to Loren Sanders and Thomas Rhodes. I wouldn't be surprised if they buy the rest of the herd. Stick to your guns with them, though. They are a couple of skinflints," Claire said.

Lena smiled. "They are men, after all."

"We will be on our way. Good luck in dealing with all this. I truly am sorry that all this bloodshed happened," Claire said as she stood.

Mrs. Welsh walked the women to the door and watched them ride away.

The men were working horses in the pasture when Caroline and Claire returned. Joey and Caleb rode their horses up to the fence and waited for the buggy to pull up to them.

"We're in the cattle business," Caroline announced.

"You might not be so excited about all of this the first time a bull chases you," Joey said.

"I'm pretty used to getting out of the way of bull," Caroline responded with a devilish grin.

"We'll need to get started on rounding up the best of Nathan's herd. I told her about Loren and Thomas. We might as well get first pick," Claire said.

"We'll have to build a chute to brand them. You can't throw a full-grown cow," Joey said.

"Well, get busy then. We didn't marry you boys for your good looks," Claire said before popping the reins and leaving the men looking at each with silly grins on their faces.

Chapter 22

October 20, 1877

The weather had turned cold again, and a gusty north wind made working downright miserable. So far, the men had rounded up thirty head of cattle and one bull and driven them back to the ranch. Getting the animals into the chute to brand proved a cumbersome and time-consuming job. Branding the fully grown cattle turned out to be a hazardous job as well. The animals would kick, rear up, and attempt to go right through the sides of the chute. When lunchtime came, Caleb, Joey, and Caroline gladly scrambled into the house. Claire had hot coffee and sandwiches waiting for them.

"I don't know if my Southern blood can stand Wyoming winters," Caleb said as he took off his coat and shuddered.

"Well, you're in for a long season then, because this is nothing," Joey said.

"I'm cold, too, but a day like today won't seem all that bad by the time winter is finished," Caroline added.

Caleb looked at the others as if they had lost their minds. "That wind is awful."

"Sit yourselves down and eat," Claire ordered.

They ate their sandwiches while making small talk. The more they warmed up, the more they chatted. Caroline wasn't in the mood to go back out into the cold.

She decided to prolong the meal by waiting until everyone had finished eating before discussing the cattle herd.

"We need to get the rest of the cattle selected and branded before we lose first pick," Caroline said.

Joey stretched his neck and looked at Caroline in surprise. "You're welcome to ride with us. Dan and I are the only two who know anything about cattle. The rest of our bunch barely knows one end of a cow from the other. That herd is scattered everywhere. A lot of them are just skin and bones and not worth owning."

"I'm trying to learn," Caleb said a bit defensively.

"Well, it shouldn't take you long to double your knowledge," Joey said with a grin.

"Maybe we should send everybody out and drive all the cattle they find to Hoover Valley. You and Dan can select from all of them at once that way," Claire suggested.

"That's probably a good idea. I never thought the cattle would be strewn about like they are," Joey said.

"We don't pay you to think—just work," Caroline said.

"I'm starting to think I liked you better before Caleb came alone and you were just hateful instead of witty. Making you mad was easier work than matching wits with you," Joey said.

Caleb grinned. "I'm the man that put a smile on her face," he teased, causing everyone to laugh at his unexpected bold behavior.

Claire began clearing dishes from the table. "This cold weather must have everybody feeling frisky. How is Levi working out?"

"Thank goodness that boy is a quick learner, because the only thing he knew how to do was ride a horse. We've got him riding and roping now, and he's getting pretty good at it. He'll be a top-notch hand before I'm done with him," Joey said.

"Yes, Joseph, I'm sure you're the only one capable of imparting wisdom to the young man," Claire said sarcastically.

"The way I'm treated in this home is liable to drive me back to the bunkhouse," Joey said.

"I doubt that. You have that itch just about as bad as Caleb does. You're just a little more subtle about it than he is," Claire said.

Joey's face began to flush. He stood and put on his hat. "We better get back to work. It's too windy in here for me," he said as he winked at Claire.

A knock on the door brought an end to the tomfoolery.

"I'm about half-afraid to answer that with the way things have gone lately," Claire said as she headed toward the front of the house.

"Mother, don't talk like that," Caroline warned.

As she opened the door, Claire said, "Captain Willis, what a surprise. Come in and warm yourself."

"Thank you, Mrs. Clemson."

The captain stepped into the house stiffly, as if his limbs were partially frozen. His ears and nose were bright red, and he shuddered from the sudden change of temperature.

The others joined Claire and the captain in the parlor.

"Is this about Cedric Bell? Is he making trouble about Levi and Bluebird again?" Claire asked.

"No, ma'am, it isn't. Are any of you aware of Paul Myers? He's a bounty hunter, and Frankie Myers's brother," the captain asked as he rubbed his hands together to warm them.

"Joey and I have crossed paths with him. I guess we know where this is headed," Caleb answered.

"He's been making a ruckus around town, asking about the killings at the Horn ranch. I think we all agree that that is a hornet's nest that doesn't need poking. He came by to see me. I told him that the army is not in the business of aiding bounty hunters and that he was on his own," Captain Willis said.

"What are you suggesting?" Claire asked.

"Oh, I'm not suggesting anything. I'm not in the habit of digging into people's past unless they give me a reason to do so. Nobody here has given me cause for such, but if this Myers fellow comes up with reasonable information that somebody is a fugitive of the law—well, the army would be powerless to intervene. I've known most of this family a long time and I think I'm a pretty fair judge of character about the rest of you. I sure would hate to see this family broken apart because some varmint is hell-bent on revenge. Excuse my language. Personally, if it were me, I would remedy the situation before it became a problem," the captain said.

The room became eerily silent except for the relentless ticktock of the clock on the mantel.

"Thank you, Captain Willis. You were always a good friend to Jackson and to this family. I do appreciate you coming all the way out to the ranch on such a cold day," Claire said.

"I was never here," the captain said, winking.

Claire scurried into the kitchen and returned with a jar of honey. "Take this home with you. I'm sure your wife and children will enjoy it."

"Thank you, ma'am. Get to training me some horses," Captain Willis said. He tipped his hat before leaving.

"What are we going to do?" Caroline asked as soon as the captain was out the door.

"You and Claire are not going to do anything. The less you two know about all this, the better off all of us will be. Caleb and I are going to go take a walk and figure this out," Joey said.

"Joey, this concerns all of us," Caroline said.

Claire took her daughter by the arm. "Joey is right. This is for the men to handle. Come on in the kitchen with me and help me finish cleaning up," she said as she led Caroline out of the room.

The men put on their coats and turned up the collars as they stepped out into the brisk air. They chose to head down the driveway to avoid the other ranch hands. As they walked, snow started spitting from the sky in big, wet flakes, forcing them to pull the front of their hats down low. To the north, the mountains were getting the brunt of the storm and only appeared as dark silhouettes.

Joey shoved his hands into his coat pockets and drew his arms in tight against his body. "That day I saw Myers in the saloon, he tried to get me to turn on you for a cut of the reward. I played dumb and told him I'd try to get you to talk."

"Oh my. He really will try anything. He and Frankie must have made quite the pair in their youth," Caleb said as he flipped away a drip from his nose.

"He's bad news for sure. I know I can lure him to the ranch. I say we get him out here and kill him. We can make the body disappear," Joey said.

"Joey, we can't just murder him in cold blood. What would that make us?" Caleb asked.

"Caleb, he's going to figure out who you are. If you intended on letting yourself get caught, you might as well have stayed in Tennessee. We both killed indiscriminately in the war to preserve the government that each of us fought for. I don't see that this is much different. You're fighting to preserve yourself this time," Joey said.

They walked on for several steps in silence.

"You get him out here. Then I'll challenge him to a gunfight," Caleb said.

"You're not a professional gunfighter. He might be good with a gun," Joey argued.

"It doesn't matter. Neither of us has ever killed anybody that wasn't trying to kill us or Caroline. And you've seen me in a gunfight. I'm pretty good," Caleb said.

"Yes, you are, but that doesn't mean Caroline won't end up a widow. If something happened to you, it just might kill her, too. I guess Claire and I will have to deal with that if you get yourself killed."

Caleb reached over and rubbed the leather bracelet he wore around his wrist. During his escape from Tennessee, he had encountered a strange old woman in Missouri who had given it to him. Alice had seemed mystical, able to know his past and future. She had made a lasting impression on Caleb, and he thought of her often. "Alice was right. I did have better days ahead. Let's hope she meant for a long, long time," he said.

Joey looked over at Caleb, grinned, and shook his head. "I swear that if you get yourself killed, I'll bury you ass-end up so I can stomp on it every time I visit your grave."

Chapter 23

October 21, 1877

The morning after Captain Willis's visit, Caleb and Joey decided they would wait another day to deal with Paul Myers on account of it being Sunday—there wouldn't be any chance of the wanted posters arriving by mail. Much to the disappointment of the ranch hands, Joey chose to spend the day rounding up all of Nathan's cattle that they could find. The weather hadn't improved any from the day before, so the crew bundled up for the ride amid grumbling about having to work on a Sunday. Joey paired everybody up and assigned them all areas to check.

"Do you think you can manage by yourself?" Caroline asked Joey. "If you do, I could see if Bluebird wants to ride with me. We could head farther east from your spot. We'd cover more territory that way, and we could help you if you have trouble moving cattle on your own."

"What makes you think Bluebird would want to be out in this weather?" Joey asked.

"I just figure she'll jump at the chance to get out of that cabin for a while," Caroline replied.

"I think she'd like that," Levi said.

"I'm good with it if she wants to," Joey said.

Caroline jogged to the cabin and knocked. Bluebird answered the door wearing one of her new dresses.

"Caroline, good morning."

"Good morning, Bluebird. We're going out to round up cattle. I thought maybe you would like to ride with me," Caroline said.

"Yes, very much," Bluebird replied excitedly. "I have nothing to do here. I go change."

Bluebird emerged from behind the partition wearing her deerskin dress, leggings, and an old buffalo coat that looked as if it had seen better days.

"That should keep you warm," Caroline said.

"Yes, for a long time. I wear it the night they steal me," Bluebird said.

Levi had already saddled the horse that had belonged to Ellis on the assumption that Bluebird would not refuse a chance to ride.

The group traveled off the ranch together and then split up and headed toward their assigned areas to scrounge for cattle.

Once they were off by themselves, Caroline asked, "So, Bluebird, are you happy living on the ranch?"

Bluebird looked at Caroline suspiciously, wondering if there was some hidden meaning behind the question. "Yes, very happy. My life best since a little girl."

"Good. I'm happy to hear that. You deserve to be happy. Does Levi like it here, too?"

"Yes, very happy. Joey good for Levi. I think like a father," Bluebird replied.

Chuckling, Caroline said, "For a man that never had children, he sure has a lot of us who think of him as a father figure. Caleb would give his life for Joey. I guess I would too—but I'd sure never tell him that. He has a high enough opinion of himself as it is."

"Is wedding good?" Bluebird asked.

Caroline paused a moment as she deciphered Bluebird's question. "You mean marriage. Yes, my marriage is very good. I've never been happier. Thank goodness I never succeeded in running Caleb off like I tried. Those days seem like a lifetime ago, and I was a different person then. How are you and Levi doing?"

Bluebird grinned. "Levi fine man and he treat me good. He want me in bed all the time," she said with a laugh.

After a fit of giggles, Caroline said, "Caleb is like that, too. If we didn't live with Mother and Joey, I think he'd be chasing me all over the house."

"My mother said keep a man tired and he stay home."

"I think your mother was probably on to something there. Doesn't sound like either one of us have anything to worry about then."

"We maybe have babies play together."

"That certainly could happen. We better pick up the pace, or the men will accuse us of loafing," Caroline said as she pressed Buddy into a fast trot.

The women rode for a couple of miles through rocky terrain scattered with pine trees until they reached some rolling hills with plenty of good grass. As they topped a hill, they spotted a herd of cattle.

"I'll see if they have Nathan's brand on them," Caroline said.

They rode in a circle around the herd. All of the brands that Caroline could see were the Horn markings. She did a quick count and tallied sixty-two head of cows with their spring calves, and two bulls. One of the bulls snorted loudly and pawed the ground with its hoof, sending dirt flying through the air. He let out a loud bellow and turned so that he faced the riders.

"These the ones?" Bluebird asked.

"Yes. We'll get them moving," Caroline said as they positioned themselves on the east side of the herd.

The women started yelling and whooping to get the herd moving. As the cattle began stirring, the troublesome bull held his ground. He pawed the dirt again and let out a bawl. With agility that belied his size, the bull charged Caroline. Her horse had plenty of experience as a cutter with mustangs, so at Caroline's touch of the reins he deftly maneuvered out of harm's way. The bull swung its rear around and rushed toward Bluebird. She tried to turn her horse, but the animal hesitated at the sight of the charging bull. At the last moment, the horse bolted to the side—but not before the tip of the bull's horn gashed the gelding's hindquarter. The horse jumped straight into the air with all four legs off the ground and landed stiff-legged. After running a few steps with the bull in pursuit, the gelding began kicking up its rear with each step. Bluebird grasped the saddle horn in a death grip as her balance in the saddle became more precarious with each buck. The next kick sent her sailing through the air.

"Bluebird," Caroline screamed before the Indian woman had even hit the ground.

Bluebird landed facedown in the dirt. Her body bounced off the ground like a ball before coming to rest. With her face pressed against the soil, she moved her arms as if she were swimming. The bull made a lunge at the riderless horse and then turned toward Bluebird.

Caroline raced Buddy in between the beast and her friend. The bull charged Caroline. She moved her horse out of the way. Then she hastily cut Buddy back in front of the bull to keep him occupied.

"Are you hurt?" Caroline yelled.

Bluebird managed to get into a sitting position. Caroline stole a quick glance over her shoulder at the woman. Bluebird looked dazed and confused. The bull charged Caroline again, and she repeated the maneuvers to avoid the animal's charge while keeping him away from Bluebird.

"Bluebird, say something."

"I'm sorry."

"Ah, to hell with this," Caroline said as she managed to get the bull to turn. She pulled her Winchester from the scabbard just before the bull charged her. Buddy again danced to the side. By the time the bull spun to face her one more time, Caroline had a bead on him. She squeezed the trigger, sending a bullet into the animal's skull. The bull let out a bellow and swung his head wildly. Caroline fired again, dropping the bull to his knees before he finally toppled over. He continued kicking wildly until the last bit of life drained from him.

"I'm coming," Caroline shouted as she jumped from her horse and almost fell in her rush to get to Bluebird.

"I'm sorry," Bluebird repeated.

Caroline squatted next to Bluebird and grasped the woman's shoulder while looking into her eyes to see if they would focus. "Where are you hurt?" she asked.

"I'm just banged," Bluebird said as she patted her coat. "Coat make soft."

"Not that soft," Caroline said as she brushed dirt from Bluebird's cheek. "Can you walk?"

Bluebird started to rise to her feet with Caroline's assistance. Once she stood, she sucked in a deep breath and exhaled slowly. Caroline released her grip on Bluebird's arm, and the Indian woman took a couple of tentative steps.

"I'm good," Bluebird said.

"Are you sure?"

"I be fine."

The overwhelming relief at seeing that Bluebird was only shaken up caused Caroline to become emotional. She embraced Bluebird and patted her back.

"You scared me to death. I thought that bull was going to get you."

"Thank you. You saved me. You my friend."

"Of course I'm your friend," Caroline said. She turned away before she began crying. "Let me see if I can catch your horse."

Caroline strolled right up to the animal. The scared horse seemed content to be captured. The wound on the hip didn't look deep enough for concern, so Caroline walked the gelding back to Bluebird.

"More bruises," Bluebird said, managing a smile.

With a little push from Caroline, Bluebird climbed onto the saddle.

"We better get you home," Caroline said.

"No, I come to work. We drive cows," Bluebird said as she turned her horse toward the cattle.

The herd had drifted about a hundred yards, then stopped. The women resumed driving the cattle up the hill toward where they had first observed the herd. At the top of the rise, they spotted Joey coming at a hard lope.

"I heard the shots. What happened?" Joey asked as he pulled his horse to a hard stop.

"We owe Mrs. Welsh another ninety dollars. I had to shoot a bull. He charged us," Caroline said.

Grinning, Joey said, "See, I know what I'm talking about. I warned you about those bulls."

"This isn't funny. Bluebird got thrown from her horse and that bull tried to get her," Caroline said.

Joey glanced over at Bluebird and noticed her disheveled appearance. "Are you hurt?"

"I'm sorry."

"Bluebird, quit apologizing. You have nothing to be sorry for," Caroline said.

"You poor little thing. You've certainly had a time of it," Joey said.

"We drive cows. I be fine. We don't tell Levi until tonight," Bluebird said.

They drove the herd to Hoover Valley. Caleb and Reese were there with the forty head they had found. Dan and Nils showed up a little later with another herd.

"Okay, let's go out and see if we can find some more of these marvelous bovines so Dan and I can pick out our herd. Just remember—if you decide to hang somebody for this big idea, Caleb is your man," Joey said.

By early afternoon, the crew had rounded up close to two hundred head of cattle with their calves and five bulls. Once a cow was selected, separating her from her calf proved to be nearly impossible in the wide valley, so Joey gave up on the idea. He and Caroline decided they would just buy the calves and fatten them for market. Dan and Joey argued over which two bulls to pick for a good ten minutes until Joey finally gave in to the ranch hand's reasoning.

"Let's get this herd home and call it a day," Joey said.

The crew drove the cattle back to the ranch and into a fenced pasture. Claire saw them ride in and walked out to the barn.

"I have supper ready for everybody," Claire announced.

"Bless you, ma'am," Dan said.

Levi noticed Bluebird climbing stiffly off her horse.

"What's wrong with you?" Levi asked.

Caroline decided to take it upon herself to explain what had happened. Claire's maternal instincts kicked in as she heard the story, and she moved to Bluebird's side to comfort her.

"Caroline save me," Bluebird added.

The comment caused Caroline to blush. She busied herself with unsaddling Buddy.

After the horses were put up and fed, Claire said, "Let's get inside the house. You all look frozen." She then shepherded the crew toward the house.

Claire had a humongous pot of beef-and-potato stew cooking on the stove. She filled bowls and placed them in front of each of the weary crewmembers. At first, only Claire brought any enthusiasm to the meal, but as the food warmed the others, they began to laugh and tease each other. By the time second helpings were being chowed down, Joey was entertaining the group with stories that nobody believed for a minute, but they laughed at them all the same.

"Levi, you need to come with me," Claire said after the meal.

She led Levi into the office with its wall-lined shelves of books.

After lighting an oil lamp and turning up the wick, Claire said, "Bluebird told me you once wanted to be a lawyer. I figured you might like to read. You're free to borrow any book you like."

"Thank you, ma'am. I do get tired of reading the same three books over and over," Levi said as he scanned the bookshelves.

Claire tapped her finger on two books stacked on the desk. "These here are two law books that Jackson bought. I want you to have them."

"I couldn't take your husband's things. And besides, that was so long ago. I haven't used my mind much since them. I doubt I could make heads or tails out of them," Levi said.

"I insist that you take them. Did you know that Abraham Lincoln was a self-taught lawyer?"

"Yes, ma'am."

"You never know—we may need us a good lawyer around her someday," Claire said.

"Claire, why are you so good to me and Bluebird?"

"Maybe I think you're my ticket to Heaven," Claire said with a wink.

Chapter 24

Fort Laramie

October 22, 1877

Joey walked to the entrance of Fort Laramie Saloon and scanned the room from the doorway. He expected to find Paul Myers sitting at his usual spot, but was disappointed to see the table unoccupied. Joey strolled up to the bar and ordered a beer. He needed a drink to calm his nerves. He and Caleb had hatched plan to deal with Myers, but putting it into action had him on edge—and worried about the outcome.

"How are you doing, Joey?" Ned, the bartender, asked as he set the mug onto the bar.

"Better than I have a right to be," Joey replied before taking a sip from the glass. "Has Paul Myers been in here today?

"Nah, haven't seen him. He tied on a good one last night and about got his tail whipped. I threw him out before there was any trouble and my saloon got torn up," Ned replied.

"Maybe getting drunk on Sunday is part of his religion. I wish he'd just disappear," Joey mused.

"I doubt that. He's gunning for Caleb and won't be happy until something happens. He's made it well known that he thinks Caleb killed Frankie," Ned said as he leaned on his elbows.

"I suspect you are right."

Joey nursed his beer as he talked with Ned. He knew he was procrastinating, but he couldn't help himself. The thought of facing Myers filled him with dread. He just wanted to get back to the days where his biggest concern was whether he would ever tame some hardheaded horse.

He walked across the street to the hotel and asked for Paul's room number. As Joey walked up the well-worn stairs, they creaked. The sound made him self-conscious, and he looked to see if anybody was watching him. The hotel lobby was deserted except for the clerk who had already returned to reading the newspaper. He found Paul's room and pounded on the door twice before he heard stirring inside.

"Who is it?" Paul hollered.

Joey didn't reply. He waited until the door cracked open so Paul could see his face. "Let's talk."

Paul let Joey into the room. The place reeked of body odor and farts and appeared disheveled. Clothes and wanted posters were scattered about the room. Myers wore only his tobacco-stained, holey long underwear. Joey thought Myers looked like hell warmed over. The bounty hunter had dark bags under his eyes. He shook as he made his way to a chair and sat down.

"What do you want?" Myers asked.

"Have you ever figured out if Caleb is a wanted man?"

"No. I'm still waiting for the sheriff of Fort Smith to send me those wanted posters. Either he or the mail is taking their sweet time. I'm going to run out of money if they don't come before long," Paul replied.

"Did you spy on the ranch?"

Myers grinned. "I did."

"Why did you do it in the snow?" Joey asked.

"Because I wanted him to know I was watching. A little game of cat and mouse can get under a man's skin. I wanted him to know I would be coming. Now, why are you here?" Paul asked before grabbing a handkerchief off the nightstand and dabbing the perspiration from his forehead. He kept taking deep breaths as if he was trying to ward off the urge to puke.

"Are you still going to pay me twenty percent?"

"Gladly, to get this over with. What do you know?" Myers demanded.

"You double-cross me and you'll be as dead as your useless brother," Joey threatened.

"For God's sake, I'll pay you the money. I'm not looking to make any more enemies. This is more about avenging my brother's death than the reward. Just tell me what you know."

"I'm going to leave here soon. In about twenty minutes, head north out of town. I'll be waiting for you in the first pine grove you come to. I'll tell you who he is and where you can find him and kill him," Joey said.

"How do I know I can trust you? I think I'll go to the army and let them know where I'm headed," Myers said.

Joey drew his gun, pulled back the hammer, and stuck the revolver in Paul's face. The bounty hunter's eyes got as big as twenty-dollar gold pieces.

"We're doing this my way or not at all. I have too much to lose if somebody figures out that I was in on this. Now decide what you want," Joey threatened.

"Sure. Sure. Get that thing out of my face. We'll do it your way," Paul stammered.

"Good," Joey said as he returned his Colt to its holster. He walked out of the room without another word.

A half hour later, Paul Myers arrived at the pine grove. He rode his horse up beside Joey's mount so that the two men were face-to-face. Joey caught a whiff of whiskey on the bounty hunter's breath. The drink seemed to have helped Paul's hangover. He no longer looked as if he might pass out.

"So what's the story?" Myers asked.

"He has a two-thousand-dollar bounty on his head— dead or alive," Joey lied.

"Well, what's his name?"

"I'll tell you afterward. I don't want you to get any ideas about eliminating me beforehand," Joey said.

"You sure are an untrusting soul. You must really want that money to put yourself through this much strain."

"No, I really want Caleb out of my way. He's going to ruin everything I had planned. I should have never let Caroline hire him just because he gave her the vapors," Joey said.

"Whatever. Just show me the way."

"Happy to."

They headed north. The air still felt chilly, but the wind had calmed during the night, making the weather seem pleasant for riding compared to the previous day. About a mile before reaching the ranch, they veered toward the northwest.

"So what do you have planned?" Myers asked.

"I have Caleb fixing some fence. We can approach him from the cover of trees. As long as you can shoot a rifle, you'll have any easy time of it," Joey answered.

"Aren't you worried your wife will get suspicious about where you're at?"

"Nah. All she knows is that I went to the gunsmith shop today. You just need to make sure everybody believes that the sheriff at Fort Smith gave you his name. You're going to have to haul the body back to Tennessee," Joey answered.

"For that kind of money, I don't mind. I can get back to Arkansas pretty quickly from there."

They reached a pine grove, and Joey stopped his horse. "This is the place," he said, dismounting.

Paul followed his lead. As he reached to retrieve his rifle from the scabbard, Caleb emerged from the pines.

"You won't be needing a rifle. Your revolver will do," Caleb said.

In a befuddled voice, Myers said, "What? What is this?"

"I'm tired of you making trouble for me. I could have killed you from the pines, but I'm going to give you a fighting chance. One way or the other, this is ending today," Caleb said as he moved his hand close to his revolver.

"I'm not no gunfighter," Myers said as he backed away from his horse. He looked around as if he were contemplating trying to make an escape.

"Neither am I. That should make for a fair fight," Caleb said.

Paul turned his head and looked at Joey. "You tricked me."

"That I did. You let greed and revenge make you gullible and careless."

"Who are you?" Myers demanded as he turned toward Caleb.

"Well, you were right. I'm a fugitive. My name is Caleb Berg. I have a thousand-dollar bounty on me in Tennessee. It's yours if you kill me."

Joey eyed Myers. He thought the bounty hunter looked scared and rattled, like he might make a run for it at any moment. Slipping the thong off the hammer of his Colt, Joey stood ready for whatever happened. He might have reluctantly agreed to allow a fair fight between Caleb and Myers, but he had no intention of allowing the bounty hunter to leave alive if Caleb lost. Paul Myers would be a dead man one way or the other.

"And I did kill your sorry excuse of a brother. Come on, Paul, go for your gun. Or are you as big a coward as your brother?" Caleb taunted.

Myers made a clumsy grab for his revolver. He struggled to clear the leather. Caleb calmly but quickly drew his Colt and sent a bullet ripping into Paul Myers's chest. Paul looked down at his wound as he finally freed his gun from the holster. His knees buckled, and he went down on them. He made one last attempt to raise his gun. Caleb fired another round into the bounty hunter, dropping him dead on his face. As he holstered his gun, Caleb looked over at Joey.

Joey let out a sigh that sounded as if he completely emptied his lungs of air. "Good shooting. I'm sure glad that is over with. Let's get his body over his horse and get out of here."

"I feel like a murderer," Caleb said as he walked toward the body.

"Well, stop it. It's not as if you killed a sheriff. He was a good-for-nothing lout, just like his brother. As far as I'm concerned, you made this world a little better place to live. I'll not lose any sleep over his death," Joey said as he bent down and grabbed Myers under the arms.

After they had Myers's body tied across the saddle, Caleb asked, "What are we going to do with him?"

"I'll show you."

Joey led the way into the mountains on a winding trail that gained altitude quickly. The horses strained to walk up the steep pass and worked up a lather. Parts of the path seemed to almost double back on itself as they rode. Caleb had never been in this area before. He kept looking around as if he were sightseeing. They reached a spot about three-quarters of the way up the mountain, where the terrain leveled off. In the middle of the flat was a six-foot-wide hole. Joey pulled his horse to a stop.

Caleb made a skeptical glance over at his friend. "You're not going to throw him down that, are you?

"We are. Come look at this thing," Joey said.

The men walked to the edge of the cavern. Joey picked up a fist-size rock and tossed it down the hole. They heard the rock bouncing down the shaft for what seemed like eternity.

"How deep do you think this thing is?" Caleb asked.

"I have no idea, but it's a long, long ways to the bottom."

"Have you done this before?"

"Jackson and I threw a horse thief down it years ago. I told you when we first met that a man has to protect what is his out here. It's always best to clean up the mess," Joey said.

Caleb rubbed his forehead and paced in a circle. "Joey, I don't know about this," he said.

"Is it really that much different than a burial? We're all going to turn to dust one way or the other. The last thing we need is for Captain Willis to have to deal with a body. None of us wants that. This ends it," Joey said.

"Let's get it over with then," Caleb said as he walked to untie the body.

They threw Paul Myers, his saddle, and all his possession down the hole. Afterward, they led Myers's horse off the mountain and turned it loose.

"What are we going to tell Caroline and Claire?" Caleb asked.

"Only that our problem is solved. That's all they need to know. Don't get any ideas about having to share everything with Caroline just because she's your wife now. You'll be doing both of you a favor by keeping this to yourself," Joey said.

"Things sure haven't been easy lately. I sometimes wonder if I'm plain bad luck."

"Don't talk like that. No, things have not been trouble-free—that's for sure. Maybe we're at the end of a bad run of luck, or maybe we're not. At least we are all alive to fight another day. Let's go home," Joey said as he nudged his horse into a trot.

Chapter 25

Langley Ranch

October 27, 1877

By the time the new cattle herd sported the Langley brand, the men were in ill moods over their new responsibilities. Dan had been kicked by an ornery cow and was limping around the yard. Reese only spoke to Caleb when absolutely necessary and continuously complained to Dan that if he had wanted to work with cattle he would have joined a real cattle ranch. Caleb convinced Joey to give the men the whole day off the next Saturday to soothe their feelings and get some rest.

After lunch on Saturday, Bluebird was at the house getting measured for her refitted dresses. Caleb and Levi walked in and announced a plan of going to Fort Laramie. They were intentionally vague about their reason for going. Making a hasty exit, they saddled their horses and headed toward town.

Levi and Caleb were finding they liked each other's company. Levi was the same age as Caroline, and the two men related to one another well. Caleb and Caroline had even spent an evening at the cabin playing dominoes with Levi and Bluebird.

"Do you think they'll have what we're looking for?" Levi asked.

"I think so. The last time I was in Mike's General Store, they had some Indian jewelry they'd traded for, and some other things shipped from back East," Caleb replied.

"I sure hope so. I really want to get a ring for Bluebird."

"I bet she'll be surprised. Women love that kind of thing," Caleb said.

The day was cold and overcast. A shiver traveled down Caleb's spine, and he buttoned his coat as they rode. He had begun to realize that Joey wasn't exaggerating about Wyoming winters. He wondered what lay in store for the coming months.

"You know, when I stayed at the hideout with the Shumans, I never even acknowledged Bluebird's existence. When Ellis would beat on her, I'd just look away. And it wasn't that I felt scared to do something about it—I just didn't care. I felt the same about Indians then as I do about snakes. I don't know why she ever forgave me," Levi said.

"It's because you changed. You're not that person anymore. Forgiveness is a powerful thing," Caleb said.

"But is that enough? It sure doesn't change the past, though. How do I forgive me?" Levi wondered.

"Can you keep a secret?" Caleb asked.

"That's one thing I always do."

"I'm a fugitive, too. I killed my brother-in-law in self-defense. He had given my sister a beating, so I went there to do the same to him. Kind of like when you killed Ellis. I knew I'd never get a fair trial. That's how I ended up in the Wyoming Territory. Charles didn't amount to anything, but I still hate what I did to my sister and her kid's life, even if they are probably better off now. I had to forgive myself to move on with my life," Caleb said.

"Thank you for telling me that. The difference is that I watched it happen for a year before I did anything."

"I've been around horses all my life. Back home in Tennessee, most of the yearlings were like puppy dogs by the time we started training them. We'd have an ornery one once in a while, but that was the exception. These mustangs out here are completely different animals. They have to be feral in order to survive. I learned real quickly that you have to understand the spirit of the wild horse to work with each one of them. My point is that you saw the essence of Bluebird. You came to love her for who she is. You learned not to resent her for some notion of what you thought all Indians must be like based on what happened to your family. I'd say you figured things out. You did do something about it once you did, and look where you are now. I'd say Bluebird and God have both forgiven you. Count your blessings and don't look back," Caleb said.

"I guess that it is a good way to look at things. Maybe I'll get there one of these days. You're a wise man."

Caleb let out a chuckle. "Don't give me credit. I'm just repeating what Joey told me. That man is the sage one."

"He really is a good man. I wish I'd met him a long time ago," Levi said.

"He's the best."

For the rest of the ride, the men talked about the cattle and the foals that Leif would sire in the spring.

When they reached town, they tied their horses in front of the general store.

"What can I do for you gentlemen?" Mike asked from behind the counter when the men walked in.

"We'd like to see your jewelry," Caleb said.

"Aren't you the young fellow who just married Caroline Langley?"

"I am."

"Well, you're in luck then. There's a piece here that Caroline eyes every time she comes through that door. She's even tried it on a couple of times, but she always talks herself out of splurging on it," Mike said as he walked down the counter to the jewelry case.

Mike pulled out a gold necklace with a pearl pendant and handed it to Caleb. Smiling, Caleb bounced the jewelry in his hand. He wondered when his wife, who usually preferred men's clothes, planned to wear something so fancy.

"How much?" Caleb asked.

"Five dollars."

"If we both buy something, will you knock off some?" Caleb inquired.

"Yeah, I can knock off ten percent. Everybody wants a bargain," Mike complained.

"I'll take it."

"What are you interested in buying?" Mike asked Levi.

"A ring."

"There they all are. Let me know if any of them catch your fancy."

Levi stared through the glass, looking for something that looked as if it was meant for Bluebird. He spotted a silver ring with a blue turquoise stone and pointed at it. Mike lifted out the ring and handed it to Levi.

"I traded for that from a Sioux, but I think it came from a tribe in the Southwest. Those Indians do a lot of trading among themselves. I'll take three dollars— minus your discount," Mike said.

Levi slipped the ring onto his little finger and held up his hand for a better look. "What do you think?" he asked Caleb.

"A blue ring for Bluebird. I think she'll love it," Caleb replied.

"Let's pay the man," Levi said, grinning like a kid buying candy.

Once they were out on the boardwalk, Caleb said, "I'll buy you a beer. We deserve one."

"Sounds good to me."

The saloon was packed with soldiers and cowboys. Caleb and Levi wedged into a spot at the bar, and Caleb ordered two beers.

Ned set the beers on the bar. "Good to see you, Caleb. I bet you're glad that Myers fellow just up and disappeared. They had to clean out his room. He left some clothes and whatnot."

"Maybe he finally gave up—or got a message he wasn't welcome here," Caleb said.

"I just bet he did," Ned said with a wink. "You boys enjoy your beers."

They left after a beer apiece. The saloon was just too crowded for their liking. When they arrived home, they found Bluebird playing dominoes with Joey, Claire, and Caroline.

The players were so involved with their game that they barely acknowledged Caleb and Levi's arrival.

After Bluebird had figured out the game by watching in the bunkhouse, she had developed a knack for it. Now she played with the seriousness of a professional gambler. Caleb and Levi took seats and waited until Caroline and Bluebird won the game.

"What have you two scoundrels been up to?" Caroline asked as she eyed Caleb and Levi suspiciously.

"Drinking at the saloon like any husband who wants to get away from his wife does," Caleb teased.

"I'm liable to keep you well away from me with talk like that," Caroline warned.

"I seriously doubt that," Claire chimed in.

"Mother, please."

Bluebird used her arms to pull all the dominoes toward her. "I guess men not tired enough," she said in reference to her mother's advice to keep a man tired to keep him home.

Bluebird and Caroline burst into giggles as the others looked on and wondered what inside joke the women were sharing.

"I must be too old to get asked along with you young bucks," Joey complained.

"We're together every night. I thought you might want to be the sole man of the house for a change," Caleb said.

"Yeah, like these three women would ever let me enjoy that."

"Joseph Clemson, you're the one who's had a high time today. You've clung to us like a child attached to his mother's apron," Claire said.

Joey grinned. "You don't have to tell all my secrets. I just wanted Caleb to feel guilty."

"We'll take you next time," Caleb promised.

"You'd just make me buy all the beers," Joey said.

Caleb reached into his pocket and pulled out the necklace. "I got you a present today."

Caroline took one look at the jewelry and let out a squeal. She jumped up from her seat and rushed to Caleb. "Put it on me."

"Thank goodness you wore a dress today. I'm not sure this would go well with suspenders," Caleb said as he fastened the necklace on her.

"How did you know?"

"I took one look at it and knew it was the one," Caleb said.

"Mike told you I had my eye on it," Caroline said, turning around so the others could see her wearing it.

"That's kind of what I said," Caleb said with a grin.

Caroline gave Caleb a kiss. "I could get used to this kind of treatment."

"You're going to ruin that girl. She has a high enough opinion of herself as it is," Claire said.

Levi had been watching Bluebird. She looked happy for Caroline, but he thought she seemed a little disappointed that there had been no mention of a gift for her.

"Bluebird, are you ready to go back to the cabin? I might have something for you," Levi said.

Bluebird's face lit up, and she stood. "I'm ready."

Joey gave Caleb and Levi a dirty look. "You two are in trouble now. You fools have made me look bad. I guess we know who has manure duty this week."

"You should be wise enough to buy me jewelry without prompting from the young ones," Claire said.

Joey closed his eyes, shook his head, and sighed.

As Levi and Bluebird were walking back to the cabin, Bluebird asked excitedly, "What did you get me?"

"Wait until we get in the cabin."

Bluebird grabbed Levi's hand and all but ran back to their home. Levi retrieved the ring from his pocket and proudly held it out for her to see. Bluebird covered her mouth with her hand and nodded her head in excitement.

"For me?" she asked.

"Yes, of course it's for you," Levi said as he placed the ring on her finger. The joy on Bluebird's face made him decide that it was best money he'd ever spent. He felt great about himself, and his eyes got misty.

"I never had present since I with my Laguna people. What does this mean?"

"It means you are my girl and I'm your man," Levi said as he took a seat.

Bluebird climbed onto Levi's lap and gave him a kiss before admiring her ring some more.

"We can make babies," Bluebird said.

"Well, we probably should get married first, but yeah, I hope we make babies," Levi said as he stood and carried Bluebird toward the bed.

About the Author

Duane Boehm is a musician, songwriter, and author. He lives on a mini-farm with his wife and an assortment of dogs. Having written short stories throughout his lifetime, he shared them with friends, and with their encouragement, began his journey as a novelist. Please feel free to email him at boehmduane@gmail.com or like his Facebook Page www.facebook.com/DuaneBoehmAuthor.

84864889R00131

Made in the USA
Lexington, KY
26 March 2018